THE WESTERN RAIDER:
THE LAW OF SILVER TRENT
AND OTHER STORIES

THE LAW OF
SILVER TRENT
AND OTHER STORIES

By Stone Cody

STEEGER BOOKS • 2020

PUBLISHING HISTORY

"Silver Trent Rides Back to Hell" originally appeared in the September 1939 (Vol. 18, No. 4) issue of *Star Western* magazine. Copyright © 1939 by Popular Publications, Inc. Copyright renewed © 1966 and assigned to Steeger Properties, LLC. All rights reserved.

"The Law of Silver Trent" originally appeared in the May 1940 (Vol. 20, No. 4) issue of *Star Western* magazine. Copyright © 1940 by Popular Publications, Inc. Copyright renewed © 1967 and assigned to Steeger Properties, LLC. All rights reserved.

"Gun-Doctor For the Damned" originally appeared in the July 1940 (Vol. 21, No. 2) issue of *Star Western* magazine. Copyright © 1940 by Popular Publications, Inc. Copyright renewed © 1967 and assigned to Steeger Properties, LLC. All rights reserved.

SILVER TRENT
RIDES RACK TO HELL

A WOMAN reached out from the howling crowd and clawed him, her finger nails leaving three red-muddy streaks down the lean, dust-whitened brown of his cheek. "Dirty gringo thief!" she shrieked.

Silver Trent walked on, eyes narrowed, mouth a bitter line of contempt. His hands were bound behind him.

But the howling crowd was working itself up into a mob frenzy now. A big, over-ripe red pepper sailed through the air and struck squarely on Trent's eye. A vicious-eyed, pock-marked townsman darted out in front of him and swung a wooden-heeled *zapato* in a savage, side-wise swipe. The heel caught the prisoner on the side of the mouth, so that the blood spurted. A shout went up from the crowd like that at a bull-fight before the kill.

"*Basta! Basta!*" the guards shouted "Quit it! Enough, now!"

Trent could catch the undertone of nervousness in their voices and knew the fear in them by the way they hustled him along and the roughness with which they elbowed through the crowd.

Somebody at the fringe of the mob yelled, "Hoist him up so we can have a little knife-throwing practice!"

The roar that went up at that was lower in note and more dangerous. And despite the savage fury that ran in him, Trent felt

1

Trent's horse... leaped
straight for the gunman....

the pit of his stomach chill. For this was the true mob-sound—
the many-headed, mindless, blood hungry roar which no man
may hear unmoved.

In the electric lull which followed a girl's voice cried out, lush
with scorn and hatred. "Will you end it for him so easily? Let
him eat *segundos* before he has the boon of death!"

Her meaning was untranslatable to anyone who does not
know Mexican prison fare, but it was understood well enough
by the crowd. It stopped them for a moment, not only because
of its specific meaning but also because it was symbol of the
drawn-out cruelty which they loved even more than murder.

Silver Trent's gray eyes found the speaker and recognised
her. Carmencita!

It hurt somehow, for they had been friends, and might have
been more if he had wished. Then he remembered, with a bitterly
savage grin that hell hath no fury like a woman scorned In any
case, her hatred had done him a brief favor this time....

For it had diverted the crowd's mindlessness from death to
long torture. And every stumbling step through that milling
mob brought the temporary sanctuary of the adobe jail nearer.

The girl was shouting nervously again, but the renewed roar of
the crowd drowned her out. The milling about them quickened
in tempo, grew more violent. Ahead, the adobe face of *juzgado*
showed, with two *soldados* in front, but just now the fifty yards
that intervened seemed like fifty miles.

FROM THE corner of his eyes Trent saw that the brown
of the guard's faces had gone muddy gray and their eyes were

4

the weak, nervous eyes of sick men. He knew what was in their minds.

They didn't mean to risk their hides protecting him. But they didn't know just when to give up. Their future reputation required them to bluff as long as possible; but on the other hand anything might happen in a situation like this. They might be killed, pulled limb from limb, before they could give up. These people did not love the soldiery.

Trent laughed savagely, and the *soldado* on his right cursed and slapped him viciously across the mouth.

In front, the burly *sargento* who formed the spear-point of their thrust through the crowd turned and flung him a savage glance. "Wait until we get you inside," he snarled.

But Trent could see that the anger he had aroused in them had delayed the moment when they would take to their heels and leave him to the mercy of the savage crowd. Maybe, in fact, it had insured their own deaths, just for that reason. For it had done nothing to check the mob.

They had begun to mill in from behind now, jostling the two *soldados* who acted as rear guard, so that they stepped on his heels. Somebody bumped into the guard on his left, knocking him into Trent.

"Get him now!" a nearby voice snarled.

The sergeant in front whirled, his face putty-colored, and Trent read there that he was about to give up with the jail not more than ten paces away!

And then a whiplash voice lifted from the mouth of a nearby alley way.

"Dogs and sons of dogs!" it snarled, "you are not fit to wipe his boots. Stay in your places. Let a man move toward him and—*Carrao de leche!*—I'll blow him to hell where he belongs."

Silver Trent froze in his tracks, his head snapping sideways toward the lean, blazing-eyed face of the Mexican who had spoken. It was Pablo—Pablo the Pious—whose reverence for the saints was a byword among those who knew him in his peaceable moments, just as his howling curses in time of action made the very skies pale in terror. Pablo—perhaps the best of Trent's men. And Trent saw now that he was alone.

He saw something else, too—the quick treacherous form that slid from a doorway in the alley behind Pablo. He shouted a warning as the knife whipped home, but it was too late. Pablo's body arched outward like a bow strung in agony. The muzzles of the twit sixguns in his hands tilted upward, blasting toward the skies. In front of Pablo then, a gun bellowed, the slug from it breaking the taut-arched bow of his body so that be went down as though in two pieces.

With a strangled curse Trent broke from the grip of his guards, whirling toward that fallen form.

The pock-marked man happened to be the first in his way Trent's driven toe caught him terribly in the belly, and he sunk down in a shuddering squeal of agony. Then, head down, taut-muscled shoulders driving like a football back, Silver charged the crowd.

The whistling butt of a gun hit him at the base of the brain, sending him staggering, dazed, against massed bodies before him. Rough, panicky hands seized him, dragged him back. He staggered, knowing vaguely that that blow would have killed him if he had not been going away from it, and not caring—because Pablo was dead.

That red, unreasoning thought filled him as they thrust him through the jail entrance. Pablo had seen that the mob would never have let him get as far as the jail door, and had deliberately sacrificed his life to save him. And he, hands bound, had been helpless to stop it. Damn them! He wasn't worth old Pablo's life!

Yet he was here now, being thrust safely behind the bars, while the infuriated mob surged over to trample Pablo's helpless body. **FOR MINUTES** after they had cut his hands free and clicked the lock behind him, he raged around his cell like a madman, kicking at the walls, trying to yank the iron bars from their adobe setting.

The sergeant's voice brought him finally to a degree of saneness "Damn you," the Mexican's growl came venomously, "nobody would have cared if we had failed to bring you in. Keep on this way, and I'll give you the castor oil treatment—and worse!"

The voice more than the threat jerked Silver back to full consciousness of his surroundings. He glared at the *soldado* with eyes that had gone bloodshot and were still a little the other side of sanity.

"You mangy coyote!" be snarled. "Come in reach of me, an' I'll grind your heart for *chili con carne.*"

The sergeant involuntarily stepped back a pace as abruptly, Trent's ears picked up the undertone that had been beating at them all the time. The mob was not satisfied. Pablo's death had been like throwing a pound of meat to a raging wolf-pack. The taste of raw flesh had done no more than whet their appetite.

Then, all at once, the roar subsided and swift, assured steps sounded in the guard's room outside. A full-fed, foppish Mexican in uniform came into the cell corridor, with behind him the flaunting, hip-swaying figure of a girl.

Silver Trent narrowed his eyes, a quick coolness coming into his mind. This was *El Coronel Ernesto Peirez, commandante* of this garrison hell-hole of Cala de Polvo and acting *alcalde* of the town. And Carmencita's presence with him meant trouble.

But for the moment, the *commandante* had no glance to spare for Trent. His flittering black eyes drilled at the sergeant.

"You are to be congratulated, Sergeant," he said viciously, "on getting your prisoner safely to the *juzgado*, with only one citizen killed. No doubt you will get the medal of honor—for not causing the whole town to be wiped out for the sake of a worthless outlaw!"

The sergeant summered, "I—I didn't know your excellency wanted—wanted him to be ki—"

"*Silenco!*" the *commandante* thundered. "You fool! What are you trying to do—get yourself stood before a wall? Get out!"

The sergeant stumbled hastily to the door.

"So I wasn't supposed to get here alive—that it?" Trent said grimly.

The *commandante* turned toward him—a big, paunchy man with a vain mouth and cruel eyes. He had recovered the cold suave manner he evidently liked to affect.

"My friend," he purred, "what difference does it make? You are an outlaw and your life is forfeit in any case "

"I'm an outlaw, all right. But I've never pulled anything in your town, or in your territory, for that matter. Why the sudden interest in me?"

The *commandante's* eyes narrowed and he smiled cynically. "You have money?"

"When a certain herd of cattle is sold…."

The officer laughed. "That herd is—no more, my friend."

TRENT TOOK a swift pace forward, his knuckles whitening around the cell bars. "Damn you!" he snarled. "What's happened? My men—"

The cynical, taunting laugh came again. "Some of them were unwise enough to resist the—er—certain others who had set their hearts on those cattle."

For a moment Trent's arms shook with the intensity of his grip on the bars. The corners of his mouth were white with fury. Then abruptly, the dancing girl's mocking, hating laughter rang out.

"Look at him!" she cried. "Look at the way a gringo dog behaves when he loses. And I once thought this was a *man!*"

With an effort, Trent got command of himself. In the black depths of that moment, this girl's scorn was a tonic he needed.

With his men dead or on the run, the last faint hope of getting out of this jail was gone. He guessed that it was the *commandante* himself who had hijacked his cattle. Now he wanted Trent dead, and quickly dead, without the bother, the uncertainty of a trial. By nightfall or before the mob outside would break in!

But the girl was still crying out, her words clawing at him. "Fool! Did you think to deceive me? Ah, that was it! You—you—a thing like you—" her laughter ripped out in a vicious stream. "You thought you were so wonderful that my very heart would turn to jelly at your look. You dog, you dared to tell me that you burned for me and when, to mock you, I asked if you wanted to marry me, you laughed! But it is I who laughs now."

Trent stared at her, stunned. Yet his amazement at this bald and shameless lie ran only on the top of his mind. Underneath, his stubborn thoughts still held to his situation, circling desperately about its facts and its hopelessness.

He had ridden out ahead of his herd—the herd he had rustled on the American side of the Border—to meet Pancho Clay, who was to take delivery of the cattle and make payment. He had taken Pablo with him, leaving the rest of the bunch, under command of Jim Clane, to bring the herd along.

He and Pablo had been jumped by Peirez's soldiers By what then had seemed luck, Pablo had been able to get free, and bad followed him into town, to his death.

He wondered if Clay had yet heard about the loss of the cattle and about his capture. But his savagely circling mind told him that Clay probably wouldn't be able to do anything for him, even if he knew Pancho Clay was only an agent. His boss was Al Corbett, a rancher Trent had never seen.

Corbett had a slick and almost foolproof scheme for getting rich. He owned a big spread on the American side and another on the Mexican side He hired cattle rustled from Texas into Mexico and from Mexico into Texas. His ownership of the

Mexican ranch was a secret. Pancho Clay was supposed to own it. But Clay was only his underling.

Nobody in Texas would care, even if they found out that Corbett brought wet cattle from Mexico. And if any Americano who had had cattle rustled, ever managed to trace them to a ranch run by Pancho Clay, why it would be Clay who got the blame and nobody would suspect Corbett. And blaming Clay, in Mexico, would not profit the Texas ranchers any more than it would profit the Mex *rancheros* to blame Corbett in Texas.

Is that way, Corbett was able to run two separate depots for stolen beef, without risking anything. He didn't even pay for having the cattle rustled until they were delivered to one or another of his spreads. It was Trent, or whatever Border runner was picked for the job who took the risks. But it was a certainty that nobody would get to Corbett with the news in time to save his life now.

And it was a pretty safe bet Corbett wouldn't bother, anyhow. Maybe Corbett would be glad to have Trent dead. Maybe Corbett had arranged to get those cattle at half price.

While Trent thought that, the girl's hating words clawed at him, half unheard.

"So, you burned for me, did you? Did you think I would look at you when a caballero like *El Coronel* favored me? Look now—and maybe you will know what the fires of hell are like—since that is where you are going!"

She turned and moved toward the *commandante,* her whole body a yearning invitation.

11

Peirez stared at her, then chuckled exultantly. "Little pigeon!" he murmured thickly.

Carmencita's arms went around him as his went around her. For just an instant she avoided his lips, while she said, "Look and suffer—gringo fool!" Then her rich mouth clung to the Mexican's.

And then behind the *commandante's* back her hand stretched out toward the cell bars, holding a key—a key obviously meant to fit the lock of the cell!

CHAPTER 2
MORTGAGED TO HELL

F OR ONE split second Trent stared in stunned unbelief. Then he reached an arm through the bars, straining, and took the metal from her. He palmed it and then jerked out a curse, calling her an insulting name, for the sake of Peirez.

The *commandante* whirled on him snarling, "Another word like that and I'll have you flayed before you are killed!"

Carmencita laughed savagely. "Do not mind him, *querida*. He has only done me the compliment to show that he envies you. Let him suffer."

And then, leaning adoringly on the *commandante's* arm, she led him out.

Trent's gray eyes blazed yellow with exultation. Free! He could get free with the first fall of dark. Free to find out whether or not it was Al Corbett who had double-crossed him. Free to get the money he needed worse than he had ever needed money before.

For the ten thousand dollars he would have got for that stolen herd would hare hired a certain lawyer for Magpie Myers, in jail in El Paso on a framed murder charge. There was only one lawyer in Texas who stood a chance to get Magpie off—Jury Bill O'Moore. But O'Moore came high. He wanted a five thousand dollar cash fee—in advance.

And if Jury Bill failed, then a way would have to be found to get Magpie loose from a jail that was as tough as any in Texas. And that would cost money, too.

Part of the black depression in Trent's mind had been the knowledge that if he died, Magpie would die, too. Now, suddenly, everything was different. Pablo was dead, and nothing could change that, but there was still hope now for Magpie. Things hadn't busted up entirely. He'd get out and—

A sudden thought froze him!

Ley de fuega! Was that it? Was this a trick to get him to try to escape and be shot down? He had no gun. Carmencita's hatred was more convincing somehow than her sudden help.

Outside, the growl of the crowd, silenced by Peirez' entrance and exit, had commenced again on a deeper note, and with more voices. Trent listened to it, feeling again that sudden coldness in the pit of his stomach.

Trent and the key from his pocket and took a quick step toward the door. One of the guards in the front room came to the corridor door and looked at him. The guard had his rifle in his hand and his face was a little pale, but his nervous eyes looked both triumphant and hating.

Trent knew now that there was no protection from him in this jail. Peirez' words to the sergeant had fixed that. And these soldiers were, at bottom, no different from the crowd outside. They hated Trent as they hated all gringos. And that hatred was greater because he was a known outlaw who was said to be a dangerous killer.

He didn't deserve that reputation. He had no more relation to the cold-eyed kill-crazy men who made up the number of the *hombres malos* than an eagle has to a wolverine but that wouldn't count with these Mexicans. They had their chance now to satisfy their hatred and their cruelty and they would not lose it!

Trent stood looking at the guard, cold-eyed and dangerous, until the man's eyes shifted uneasily. Outside now, the mob was surging toward the jail door, for Trent heard the sergeant's voice saying, *"Hombres! Hombres!"* in a tone of mock reproach that was almost an invitation.

A sudden thought struck him. He strode swiftly to the cell window, looking out into the yard. So far nobody in the crowd had thought to go around there. And then, in that instant, a horse came into the alley-way across the yard—a rangy, deep chested horse led furtively by a Mexican boy, who glanced hastily around him, then tossed the reins over a protruding beam that served as a hitchrack and hurriedly disappeared.

In front, there was a deep throated yell and the padding surge of bare feet charging the jail door.

Trent threw himself at the lock of the cell. The key slid in, stuck, turned, and the door swung open!

In the same moment, the cursing, yelling surge of the crowd rushed over the floor of the front office.

TRENT FLASHED down the corridor toward the side door, shot back the bolts. The crowd had checked, growling like a catamount that had missed its spring. Now, a snarling voice snapped out excitedly. "*Aquá!* There he goes!"

A shot howled down the corridor, clanged off the iron door as Trent slammed it behind him.

Then he was racing across the yard toward the horse. Back of him, in the passageway that ran past the jail, another voice yelped a warning and another gun blasted, the bullet whining viciously past Trent's head.

He lunged for the reins, whipped them over the horse's head and jumped for the saddle. Lead howled about him. The infuriated mob was issuing from the side door now. Something slammed him in the ribs like the blow of a giant sledge, so that he almost lost his seat as the spur-driven yellow horse lunged toward the alley mouth.

He held the saddle, spurs raking. In front of him, startled faces looked from the back windows of houses. Behind him, the yell of the mob was a high pitched snarl of savage disappointment.

The sharp, high-powered explosion of a rifle sounded in the mouth of the alley and the yellow horse leaped convulsively, breaking stride. Trent's jaws clenched, but the animal found his feet and before the rifle could speak again Trent had whirled him into a side street and was racing for the edge of town.

The center of town was a cauldron of seething, shouting humanity, but the mob roars were growing fainter as each reaching hoof-heat bore Trent farther from it. Yet be knew this was not the end. Pursuit was beginning now, and he had a wounded horse. His eye sought out the horse's wound—and saw that the rifle bullet had ploughed through the side of the haunch, deep enough to rake the animal's entire flank. Only a fraction of an inch had kept it from severing the cinch where it joined the saddle.

Trent continued. The bullet had missed vital portions, but already the yellow horse was favoring the left hind leg so that his pace was uneven. There was no way to tell how long he could last. And there was no other horse in sight.

He became aware suddenly that the saddle, the Winchester in its boot, and the sixguns lashed tightly about the horn were his own. For a moment, his thoughts lost their grimness and tension. Carmencita! He had been wrong to distrust her. Women were unpredictable. Yet to this little Mexican girl he owed his life as surely as he had ever owed it to anyone.

Somehow, it eased his bitterness, so that the emotion of relief was stronger than his sense of triumph at being free, at least for the moment.

He loosened the leather strings and belted the guns about his waist, the familiar feet of them giving him confidence despite the laboring gallop of the yellow horse.

Behind him—almost a mile, he judged—faint yells and shots

broke out. The pursuit, racing out of town, had caught sight of him.

HE WAS riding across a flat, mesquite-dotted land, headed toward the hills and the hideout that was his. The country was cross-hatched by arroyos, but the dust in them was so deep horseman's progress could be spotted for miles The westering sun beat at his face and chest like something tangible and heavy. It was still three hours to dusk.

He rode, trying to forget the pain in his side, trying to concentrate on every trick he knew to throw off pursuit in that country, trying to forget that every labored stride of his wounded horse brought the end nearer.

That hammering agony had grown and was growing with every stride. The instant the shock had died away the lancing pain had begun, springing outward into every part of his body and mind. And the riding didn't help it any. He could feel the gritty rub of the broken ribs with every step the yellow horse took.

Down his side, across his thigh and into his boot the blood was a warm flow, constant and undiminished, as though his life were flowing slowly and inexorably from him.

He tried to keep the knowledge of it out of his mind because he had not time to stop and do anything to check that flow. But he could not, and fear was in him because his life was seeping away and he could do nothing to stop it. He struck at the fear savagely, as a man uses his will for a club, and drove it under the surface. forcing his mind to the need to get away, to cover his trail before his horse gave out.

But his thoughts came to him through a scarlet haze.

He felt the yellow horse slow, fight to keep his pace.

"Keep your tucker up, yeller-buck," he said urgently "You stay up an' I'll get us out."

The horse seemed to hear him, and find a steadier stride. Behind him something buzzed like a tired bee, and he could hear the plop of it in the sand. Long range, but too close!

His mind cleared for a moment and he drove toward the shelter of an arroyo that ran close and straight. The hot flush of fever in his cheeks beat back at the driving rays of the sun. The ride was a nightmare, with the distorted shapes of the brush and the washes jumping at him like live and menacing monsters. And ahead, the hills, growing clearer, lifted their blue mocking shapes that surged toward him and receded endlessly.

The sun would not go down.

And yet the yellow horse held up—this rangy buckskin miracle, this blood-spurting fool of a horse that kept running, beyond belief, without end.

And in much the same way, Trent's trail-cunning kept ripping through the deepening, whirling fever haze of his mind.

But the red haze darkened; the yellow horse faltered, stumbled, slowed.

Silver said hoarsely, "Steady, boy."

But it got through to his mind that this, after all, was the end. All his trail-sense had failed, because there were hoof-beats driving toward him. He had failed after all to throw off the pursuit. Somehow, he must have circled backwards, because these riders were coming on him from ahead. And his eye-sight was failing, because it was almost dark.

He dragged the Winchester from its saddle boot.

Abruptly, the yellow horse went down to his knees then rolled to his side. Trent got clear instinctively, and struggled painfully to his feet, the Winchester lost, to find himself confronted by half a dozen riders. The leader stared at him frozenly for a moment and then his hand lashed toward his gun.

TRENT HAD been staring at him, almost blindly, yet recognizing him vaguely as someone he had seen before. A lean, wolfish man with a scarred face and pale blue eyes under thick black brows.

The movement of the man's hand toward his gun set off Trent's own gun-hands. His Colts whipped out, in blurred, gunmetal streaks, so fast that the lean man's gun had not cleared leather before they were leveled at his middle.

The lean man froze, and the five riders with him were sudden marble statues.

And then, a little hoarsely, the lean rider spoke, "Why—hello, Silver. Hell, I didn't recognize you at first!"

Trent, swaying, half-blind, peered through the gathering darkness.

"Hullo, Clay," he muttered. "I—I didn't know you, either."

It came to him suddenly that this dusk not from weakness but was because the sun had gone down at last. And the pursuit?

He started to turn to look behind him, but some vague instinct checked him, and he set his ears to listening while still facing this crowd. There was no sound. Dazedly, he wondered if he had thrown Peirez' crowd off, and when.

Uncertainly, his guns still in his hands, he stared at Pancho Clay and his men. Why were they so rigid and silent. He felt danger in it, for there had been something in the eyes of this scar-faced man, some secret murder....

A voice lifted sharply, grating. "Take it easy, polecat! What the hell were you doin' reachin' for that gun?"

Trent's head snapped sideways, his brain clearing suddenly. Jim Clane! The voice was not to be mistaken. Nor the enormous loom of the great-shouldered form beside him.

He laughed abruptly, weakly, feeling the feebleness running in his knees and knowing all at once that all he wanted was to lie down and rest, as his horse had done.

"Hi, Jim," he said huskily, "Hiya, Lars!"

But Jim disregarded him. "Talk up, you mangy coyote," he snarled at Pancho. "Why were you reachin' for that gun?"

Pancho Clay forced an uncomfortable laugh. "Hell, Jim," he said, "I didn't know who it was. He come out of the dark an'...." He shrugged.

"Not so dark as all that," Jim snapped. "Listen, half-breed—one more mistake like that will be plumb fatal."

It was too dark to see Pancho's face flush, but it seemed to Trent that he could see his features turn darker even in the gloom.

He said curtly, "Quit it, Jim. Take it easy...."

Clane shot a quick glance at him, but when he spoke, his voice was softer. "It's your play Silver. Only—"

"Any man can make a mistake," Trent said.

"Why, hell, yes!" Pancho Clay's voice was hearty. "Silver come lungin' at me out of nowhere. What the hell would I be drawin' on my own pardner for? You think I'm loco?"

It was Silver's turn to stiffen. "Well, hardly pardner," he said drily.

Clay shrugged. "Have it the way you like. But anyway, we got a use for one another."

THE DARK landscape whirled about Silver Trent coming to sudden and bewildering halts. And his thoughts followed, it seemed, the cycle of his vision—sometimes whirling and vague, sometimes sharply clear.

He waited until the halt came and then said, "... *Was* useful. The herd's gone—rustled."

Clay gave a convincing start of surprise "What do you mean?"

Silver told him. Told him also of his escape from jail and the posse that must be even now on his trail.

Clay cursed sulphurously. In the end, he sat thoughtful. "Damn bad," he muttered, "but there's a way out. I can't pay you for the herd you lost. But Corbett can pay you for a new one. Old Bautista has made a gather of his cattle for the market. They're ripe to be taken. It's hardly a day's ride from here. But they got to be taken right away."

Silver said quickly, "Where? Where are they?"

Then the whirling hit him and he felt Jim Clane's hand on his arm. "We got to talk this over," Jim growled. "Come on, Silver. You, *hombre,* keep your men where they are—an' wait."

He led Silver away, sat him down in a clump of brush.

"Listen, *amigo*," he whispered. "You're bad hit. Stall this side-winder off. I'd trust this Clay about as far as I could throw a range bull by the tail. I don't want him to know how bad you are off, or the fact that we got none of the gang to back us up. Lars is hit, too, an' if Clay knew you was as bad as I know you are, he might have the nerve to jump us. It would be a good time for it."

Silver said thickly, "Don't be a fool, Jim. What makes you think Clay would jump us? He's got everything to lose by it."

"Mebbe," Jim Clane growled. "But I don't trust that breed."

"Trust him or not," Silver said through clenched teeth, "we got to go get those cattle."

Jim Clane cursed. "You're loco, *hombre*. Those of our crowd that ain't dead are scattered. Lars is bad enough hit to need a rest. An' you—you're done up plenty."

Silver's hands clawed at the dust beside him, the sudden flush of his anger burning his cheeks. "Listen, Jim," he snarled. "Do you think you've begun to rod this gang? By God, we need money for Magpie, an' this is a chance to get it. I say we get those cattle, an' I don't want excuses, I want action!"

Jim Clane crouched rigid beside him, temper tightening his jaw muscles. But when he spoke his voter was quiet, even placating. "Hell, Silver—you know I ain't tryin' to take charge. I—"

Lars Johanssen's booming murmur cut him off. "W'at th' hal, Jim! Me, I got one of dose little scratches like a gal make wit' a pin. We leave Silver somewhere an' we take dose cows like notting. Yust some greasers to fight. Sa-ay, what you excited about? You scared from greasers?"

22

Jim Clare whirled on him, his voice burring with fury. "Scared? Why you damn—"

Silver cut him off sharply. "Quit it!"

He was holding back the hot whirling of his head by the sheer hammering force of his will now, and he kept on holding it back while they talked again with Pancho Clay.

WHAT THEY planned was madness, and it is possible that Trent would never have tried it if he had been his normal self. The hills were sure to be swarming with Peirez' men. It would be luck if they even got through to where the cattle were. And they would have to use inexperienced vaqueros—natives who could be counted on to do the work of driving cattle, but who would probably be useless where fighting was needed.

Well, Silver told himself stubbornly, the three of them would be enough for the fighting.

He thought that out while tossing in his blankets that night, with the fever burning through his body, and the grating of his smashed ribs only partly checked by the bandages Jim and Lars had wrapped about him. And in the morning he had only enough consciousness in his semi-delirium to give the orders for the raid.

There were two days and two nights and again a day which were pure red nightmare after that. He had a vague recollection of riding through hill country, the hazy scarlet of his mind imbued with the hunted wolf notion of slinking through unseen.

And there was a night of raving tossing, during which he talked with old Magpie in his cell and said, "Old-timer, you're out now. It's done. You're out. Depend on that." And all the while he kept stabbing a Mexican bayonet into the ribs of Colonel Peirez and his sergeant, to the wild applause of Carmencita, who swam about his head, swooping and splitting the night with scornful laughter.

And there was a dawn where men shot guns at him and he shot in return and cattle stampeded, and he thought that bullets were not needed because the grating ribs in his side would pierce his lungs whether lead found him or not.

All this with moments of sanity when he gave orders in the old way and saw very clearly what was to be done.

The intervals of clarity were frequent enough for him to bring fifteen hundred wild longhorn Mexican steers through arroyos roundabout to the Border.

He remembered Jim and Lars, up in the hills, trying to make him lie up and rest, and Jim snarling, "You damn locoed fool, you'll kill yourself and run all of us into hell, the way you're going!"

There was the time, too, when some profound instinct or intuition made him reject both Jim's and Lars' insistence that they take a certain canyon trail instead of the backwinding ravine he himself chose. After an hour, Jim rode up onto a high rock from where he could overlook the other trail and found its exit blocked by a company of Peirez' *soldados*. Jim came riding down to him with his eyes fierce green under his red thatch and his jaw set like a twisted red oak knot, and cursed him, saying, "Nobody but a damn bat-eared, stubborn fool like you could be right even when he was plumb out of his head with the fever."

And there was some irrational trouble with Lars who believed that he could go over and take that company single-handed.

Lars was no fool, and there was no batter or sounder heart on earth, but in his semi-delirium Trent remembered that Lars had a profound, unreasoning conviction that bullets could not hurt him and that all Mexicans, except his personal Mexican friends, were so many lice to crack between his great thumbnails. So he had said, cunningly, that he was afraid of a worst ambush later on, and wished that Lars would stay with them. But of course, if Lara wanted to desert now....

And Lara had cursed in Scandinavian.

Then after days there was the river, with Texas on the other side, just at dusk.

The peak of the fever had overtaken Silver the day before and had subsided. His moments of clarity were greater now, and even though the bone did grate so that he thought his ribs would wear too smooth to knit, he had begun to believe that he would get through. The heat in his cheeks and the red in his mind were less and there was a weakness in him which felt like the beginning of convalescence.

He gave the order for Jim and Lars to stay on the Mexican side, flanking the herd to keep it straight across this deserted and little known ford, while he rode point. The Mexicans could handle the drag and the flanks of the herd as it came down to the water.

Then in the dusk he rode down to the ford....

CHAPTER 3
A DEAD MAN RIDES AGAIN

BEHIND HIM, the first steers snorted, hesitated and then plunged into the water. In the deepening dusk he rode across and laughed a little softly. "Here it is, Magpie," he said, "Ten thousand silver cartwheels on the hoof!"

Behind him, the herd plunged in, crossed, and took the trail he led them up toward Al Corbett's ranch. Perhaps half of them had crossed when Silver's roving eye caught a stir in the bushes beside the road just ahead. Curiously, he rode in that direction, thinking, half absently, that it was some small animal.

And then, abruptly, a gun roared in his face.

It was a miracle that the slug missed him. Maybe it was because he had just leaned sideways to get a better look at a bush that looked too dark and solid.

The shot was so close that the flash of it half-blinded him and the powder stung his face.

His horse took a panic-stricken jump sideways, swung under Silver's quick hand and then, as the spurs struck home, leaped straight for the gunman. And at Trent's right another gun flamed orange fire, the bullet whizzing past Trent's ear.

The first man came to his feet with a startled curse, flinging up his gun to fire again. But a gun was in Trent's hand by now and the muzzle flame of it lighted the man's face so that the quick dark hole between his eyes showed plain. Then the darkness closed in again.

The two shots were so close that they might have been fired by the same gun—and they were the signal for hell to break loose.

Down the line other guns broke out like firecrackers. And the ford and the Mexican shore beyond it was a blazing crackle of sudden death.

Cursing, Trent swung his horse and jumped him for the second gunman. His bullet cut the man down just as the cattle decided to stampede straight ahead.

Behind, the herd surged suddenly into frenzied, bellowing motion, following the traces of the lead steers. At the same time, they broke from the strung-out column and began to spread.

Trent, racing back toward the hammering gunfire on the other shore had to swerve aside to miss the oncoming rush. Behind him, guns sounded and lead clipped his shoulder, so that he knew that other men had been spaced along ahead of him.

His mind was a furious riot of amazement, for the first bush-whacker had been dressed in the uniform of a *Rurale*. What was one of the *Rurales* doing on the American side of the river?

It took only four jumps of his racing horse to answer that question. This was lonely country. It was unlikely that an American Border Patrol would be along here, and this was a Mexican trap. The *Rurales* had dared cross the border because they did not intend that there should be any witnesses left against them.

So much his mind took in as he raced back toward the ford, toward Jim and Lars.

His horse shied at a dark object in front and Silver saw that it was the dead body of one of the Mexicans who had ridden with the herd. Almost as soon as he recognized it, the thundering steers swept toward him, so that he had to swerve, while the sharp, pounding hoofs swept over the body of the fallen Mexican.

At the ford, the firing stopped suddenly, except for sporadic shots. And then Jim Clane's voice lifted in a high-pitched yell, "Ride for it, Silver. *Rurales!* We're cau—" The voice choked off suddenly.

In front of Silver, guns opened up and lead whined through the darkness about him. He swung his horse to the right, racing for the open country. There weren't less than two dozen guns immediately ahead of him. And there'd be others beyond the ford, and still others, surely, the other side of the herd. Bucking them would have been a stupid form of suicide

A BULLET thunked into flesh just in front of his knee and his horse screamed and went down. Trent hit rolling in the brush, his side a sudden madness of pain.

He could hear their shouts and then the quick thud of hoofs, with the faint bellow the continuing thunder of the herd's stampede.

But the stampede was still spreading and he knew suddenly that his immediate danger lay with the cattle. He got to his feet and ran desperately. Hoofs thundered down on him. Horns loomed like silvery scythes of death in the starlight. Tight-mouthed and hard-breathing, he ran, his racing feet pounding the alkali like driving pistons. There was a hot breath, on his neck, and then the dark, hurtling body swept past behind him.

He still ran then, not sure that this danger was over. Then he heard the thud of other hoofs—horses this time—and knew that he had missed one death only to invite another.

The shadow of an arroyo showed its dark chasm before him and he slid, plunging down its bank. He hit the shallow bottom hard and turned, his boots noiseless in the soft earth and ran north, away from the river. After a hundred yards, he climbed up the bank into the midst of a clump of brush and lay still.

The thud of hoofs sounded on the bank across from him and pounded on. A rider flashed up the arroyo itself, passed with his face on a level with Silver's, so that he could make out the dark oval of it and the flash of the intent eyes as the man rode.

Then on his own side, another rider hammered towards him. Silver lay utterly still, hearing the growing thud of the hoofs behind him, his back rigid yet shrinking, waiting for the driving, crippling blow between his shoulder blades or on the back of his head.

But the horse swerved, ever so slightly, snorting a little, as though he had scented the prone figure there in the brush. He did not check his stride, and his rider evidently believed that he had swerved only for the brush.

A moment later another rider passed farther off and Silver could hear the others beating the brush beyond. He lay utterly still.

Presently they began to come back, calling to one another and cursing. Again the rider in the arroyo passed him without seeing him. And finally, the man who had ridden so close to him returned.

This time he was riding even closer to the arroyo's edge and riding slow, so that when his horse snorted and shied at Silver's prone form the rider cursed, startled, and stabbed for his gun.

Trent shot to his feet, caught the horse's rein in one iron grip and the rider's arm in the other. Under the savage jerk of that hand, the *Rurale* came from the saddle with a startled squawk. Trent let him hit the ground hard, stabbed for his gun with his freed hand, and brought the barrel down with a sharp smack to the back of the Mexican's head.

A voice, twenty-five yards away, asked a question sharply and Trent said in Mexican, *"De nada!* I thought I had seen something here, but it was nothing."

He swung into the saddle and the other rider, apparently satisfied, went on.

TRENT EASED off to the right and when he felt sure that he was out of hearing he turned back, riding away from the river again. His side was a hot throb of pain and the fever flush had come back to his cheeks. It seemed to blaze outward, burning his skin and then to draw inward setting up a conflagration in his mind.

He had not had much time to think before but now that he had, his thoughts didn't help the fever any. This had been a trap all right. The *Rurales* had meant to kill or capture at any cost, and he, Trent, had escaped only by luck.

But who had set the trap? Only two men knew where the cattle were to cross in all that lonely length of Border—Pancho Clay and Al Corbett. Pancho had sent a letter by special messenger to Corbett, telling him of the deal and warning him to have the money ready. Trent had seen the letter and seen the messenger ride off with it.

So either Clay had betrayed them, or Corbett had. And Corbett was a hell of a lot more likely, since Clay was only the agent. Corbett was the man that stood to gain.

Trent laughed suddenly, bitterly. An accident? Then why had the *Rurale* let the cattle get cross?

Hell no! It had been a frame-up by Corbett, working with the *Rurales*, to get his cattle for nothing, killing or jailing Silver Trent and his crowd. Nothing else could account for the *Rurales* crossing the Rio and waiting for most of the cattle to get across.

The conclusion hit Trent's mind with a ferocity of sheer anger that shook him from head to foot. His hands went to his guns, gripping them for a moment until his knuckles whitened. Then, savagely, he swung the horse's head toward where he knew Corbett's home ranch lay.

Al Corbett had made a little mistake—just a little, minor mistake that would cost him ten thousand dollars and his life.

There wasn't any doubt in the red, pain-racked riot of Trent's mind. It was pretty certain that Corbett kept his cash at his ranch. A man in his business could not wait to deal with a bank. So he would collect that money, and then he would shoot Corbett down like any sneaking, mangy, murdering coyote.

After that, he would go back and find out if Lars, as well as Jim was alive, and get them both out of whatever jail the *Rurales* had put them in. That needed fast work because they'd be condemned to death for rustling cattle. But first Corbett had to die. That was the only solution....

31

But by the time he rode up to Al Corbett's ranch house, it was somehow less clear. At least the details were. But the conclusion was fixed enough. Corbett had to produce ten thousand dollars and then die. There wasn't much room or any need for any other thought.

A purely animal caution made him pull down the pace to a walk and ride into the ranchyard softly. He left his horse under the spread of a big cottonwood at the corner of the house and walked toward the veranda steps. But he did not bother to look into a window. He merely crossed the veranda and shoved the unlocked door open, and strode into the room with a flat, hard step.

ODDLY, THE door opened directly into the living room of the ranch house, but he thought nothing of that, any more than he had troubled to think that the house itself was unusually small for that of a prosperous dealer in stolen cattle.

A wiry, brown-eyed man, with a solid chin and a graying mustache over a firm mouth looked up, startled, at his entrance. In the doorway to what was evidently the kitchen, a girl with brown hair and a lovely, oval face looked at him, her hands going suddenly to her throat.

He backed up against the door closing it and standing there, narrow-eyed, annoyed by the fact that there was a girl there, but taking a wicked pleasure in the sight of Al Corbett's fear-widened eyes.

The man, he thought, was guilty as hell, else he wouldn't be scared the first time anyone popped into his doorway.

He did not think of how he, himself, might look—the apparition he made—hatless and disheveled, his shirt bloodstained, his face scratched by mesquite thorns. Fever-flushed and staggering, he looked like a drunk with sheer murder in his graygreen, slitted eyes.

Nor did he realize, in that moment, that single silver lock sweeping back across his black hair—the lock which had given him his name—identified him instantly as an outlaw, a killer whose gun-speed was notorious. He did not know that he was taken in that split second for what he was—Silver Trent—and on the kill!

His hands lifted a little, pointing the twin muzzles of his guns at the man in the chair. "You low-down, double-dealing polecat," he rasped. "You made a bad mistake this time. I didn't die. Get up on your laigs, coyote, and grab ten thousand dollars out of your safe before I blow the shine out of you."

The eyes of the man hardened. "You're loco, *hombre*," he said slowly. "What safe? You've come to the wrong food store if you want dinero like that."

THE GIRL in the doorway started to move, backing out toward the kitchen. Trent's eyes drilled at her. "Stay where you are, girl," he rapped out. "Try to move out for help an' I'll kill him where he sits."

The girl froze, her face bloodless and still, as though she thought that the movement of an eyelash might bring the threat into execution.

Al Corbett said, "Stay where you are, daughter. This gent's made some kind of mistake. We'll get it straightened out."

"You're damned right we will," Silver snarled. "Get the money I'm in a hurry."

"Listen, friend," Corbett said patiently, "I don't know what you mean or what you're after. If you think there's money here, look around you. I'm only—"

"You're only a murderin' sidewinder," Trent ripped at him. "Now, listen, Corbett. You had me jumped back in Mexico and a damn good man died because of it. Missin' me then, you had me jumped here at the river. An' that failed. I'm aimin' to kill you anyway. So just tell me one more lie an I won't put it off."

The rancher sat forward in his chair, in a sharp, angry movement of impatience. "You fool!" he snapped. "Who in hell do you think you are to—"

The movement of Trent's thumb and the click of the Colt-hammer cut him off.

Sweat sprang out suddenly on his forehead and his mouth whitened under the sweep of his mustache. And Trent knew then that he had understood at last.

The girl's sharp gasp broke that instant of deadly silence. "Don't!" she breathed desperately. "You're—you're mad!"

Suddenly, surprisingly, Al Corbett relaxed, leaning back in the chair. "Go ahead an' shoot, then," he said quietly. There ain't anything I can do about it."

Treat's mouth set in a long solidly savage line and his thumb slid backwards to let the hammer fall. And then he realized, almost bewildered, that he couldn't let the hammer fall. He had killed, it was true—but only when he had to, and in a fair fight. This animal deserved to die and yet....

His eyes strayed across the room to where a gunbelt and Colt hung on the wall. "Git up an' get your gun," he said hoarsely. "I'll give you that much of a break."

Al Corbett looked at him tighted-lipped, his lids dropping a little, veiling his gaze. "No," he said softly. "I'm not goin' to ease your conscience. You'll do your murder straight, or not at all!"

There was an instant's deadly silence, during which Trent could hear the quick breathing of the girl by the kitchen door and another sound, rasping and hoarse and painful, which he realized with a shock of surprise was his own breathing.

And then a hard voice snapped. "It's not at all, I reckon. Drop your guns, *hombre*—quick!"

CHAPTER 4
FIRST AID FOR BANDITS!

TRENT'S HEAD snapped toward the window. A lean, tough looking puncher's face was there, looking over the sights of a Colt .45. Cold fury ripped through Trent. He should have killed Al Corbett minutes ago.

Instinctively, he flung himself toward the chair in which Al Corbett sat. Before he hit the floor, the gun blasted from the window, the slug tearing the muscles of his back.

And as he landed on his elbows, twisting, the door behind bunt open. He slammed a shot at the window. The bullet hit the puncher's gun; sent the man's face dropping into the darkness.

The impact of a slug hit Trent in the back, so that he rolled, the breath going out of him. Dimly, Trent made out a grizzled, narrow-eyed man standing in the doorway, his oak-knot face looking over the barrel of a smoking sixgun.

The gun in Trent's left hand bucked against his palm—and the grizzled man fell backward, spinning out of sight.

He struggled to his feet, his guns centered on Al Corbett who was racing across the room for the sixgun on the wall. Corbett's hand hit the butt and then the girl's frantic voice cried out. "Dad! No!"

Corbett's eyes looked into the caverns of Trent's twin muzzles. He froze, his face suddenly gray.

For an instant Trent swayed on his feet, his reddened eyes death freighted. Abruptly he holstered his guns. "Pull it, Corbett," he grated.

But Al Corbett stood still and somehow Trent knew that he could not kill this man unless he pulled his gun.

He groaned suddenly, as through the middle of him where the gray shock had lived, red pain was beginning. His back was wet with a spreading stickiness and from the bullet hole in the front of him blood fountained, dripping on the floor. When he breathed there was a sharp stabbing pain in his right lung.

And suddenly there was a black, overwhelming bitterness in him, a crushing knowledge that all his life had been a failure which had ended now in futility. He could not even kill the man who had brought him and hit men to their death.

Outside, a hammer of hoofs sounded, the broken sliding rhythm of it coming to his ears like a far-off drum beat of warning.

He said thickly to Corbett, "Stand away from the gun, you,"

and then he moved, staggering toward the kitchen door. The girl fell back before him, her dark eyes oddly luminous in her bloodless face.

Trent looked at her. "You—you," he said thickly. "You're a hell of a thing to come from him. You look—like a—a magnolia blossom in moonlight. But hell's got to be in you."

And then he was thrusting out the kitchen door and staggering around the house to where he had left his horse. The men who had ridden in were rushing toward the front door. He grinned thinly. They'd heard the shots, no doubt. Well, the hell with them!

He found the saddle and set the horse jumping away into the darkness. Behind him a gun-blast hit the night air. But the bullet missed!

Not that that was important. He was finished anyway.

He gave the horse its head, feeling the warm rush of the night air on his face and hearing the brush of the mesquite against his chaps and the animal's flanks.

The big stars reeled overhead, and the gallop of the horse was like the cradling of a stupid nurse rocking a child in the forward and backward jolting jerk of a straight chair.

And later there was an all-consuming scarlet of agony and, in the end, a blackness like an eternal mercy.

He thought, "Hell Magpie—I—I'm damn sorry, old-timer."

And that was his last glimmer of consciousness before the deep black whirled in....

SOMETIME AFTER that, he lay on his back, with the

feel of a sheet under his finger tips. It had been a long time, he thought, since he had felt a sheet.

A woman's face, square-jawed and queerly gentle, leaned over him. "You're all right," she said. "Don't try to talk. You've been very sick, but you're getting better now."

At some time after that there was the winkled face of an old man who clearly was the old woman's husband. And there were days afterwards when his strength grew, and he was at last able to lift one of his hands up from the sheet, and look about.

"How long have I been here?" he demanded, when the old lady next brought him his broth.

She eyed him quizzically. "What do you care?"

He said desperately, "I've got to know."

Her twinkling eyes grew grave. "Three weeks now. You were very near death."

He groaned, "My men," he muttered. "If they've been killed—"

Her old, wrinkled eyes were suddenly gentle. "Nothing is ever as bad as it seems," she said quietly. "There is nothing you can do, so you must not worry."

Later he learned that their name was Sims—Joe and Martha Sims—and that they ran a small spread of cattle and a few goats and pigs and planted some vegetables so that they were able to make a living.

"We're jest kind of holdin' on an' enjoyin' the air until the time comes to check out," the old man told him placidly. "The cattle kind of gits along by theirself, an' every onet in a while I git a neighbor to come over and help me round up a few fer the market. Long ago a gent give me a lift out of a jackpot, so don't worry—we're jest payin' up for favors received when this country was fitten for a white man to live in."

Trent grinned suddenly and felt better.

After that a day came when he could get out of bed and walk around a little. A square of mirror hung on the wall and when he got up he went and looked at himself in it. For a moment he stared, hardly recognizing the face that looked back at him—a lean, pale, bearded face with gray eyes staring at him out of deep, gaunted sockets. He looked like the ghost of himself ten years older.

And there was something queer about him. For a while he couldn't make it out, and then suddenly, he saw. His hair was all black. The wide silver jock which spread back from his forehead was gone. What the hell? A chest wound couldn't do that!

He turned to and Joe Sims standing in the doorway looking at hurt.

"You did that?" Trent said sharply.

The oldster nodded.

"Then you knew who I was."

Joe Sims nodded again.

Trent stared at him. "But why?"

Old Joe's face screwed up. He shifted the cud of his tobacco from one cheek to the other and spat placidly at a beetle which labored across the adobe floor.

"Ever hear of Bucktooth Sims?" he asked.

Trent stiffened defensively. "Yeah—I've run across him."

"Kind of helped him out, didn't you?"

"He happened to be nearby at the time," Trent growled. "It didn't cost me any trouble."

Joe Sims shifted his cud to the other cheek, hit the recovering beetle dead center and said, placidly, "Don't give me that. There ain't hardly a two-bit rancher either side of the Line that don't owe you somethin'. An' us Sims ain't forgetful."

He shot a glance at Trent's flushing face and angry eyes, cackled briefly and walked out.

Silver glowered after him and then walked back to bed. The quick thud of a horse's hoofs outside brought him sitting up.

A voice that seemed somehow familiar said, "Hello, Joe. Hello, Martha." A girl's voice. Trent-half relaxed and then tautened again.

Joe's voice said, over-heartily, "Why, hello, Gina! Long time no see."

He could catch the strain in Martha's voice too, sense their fumbling efforts to keep the visitor from coming into the house. But that proved useless. A minute later a girl appeared in the doorway of his room—a girl with brown hair and a lovely oval face—a face that looked like a magnolia blossom in the delicate flush of dawn.

Treat's heart stopped suddenly and his pulse stilled. For this was Al Corbett's daughter!

CHAPTER 5
A MAN ALONE

JOE SIMS' dry voice said, "This here's a friend of our'n, 'Gina. Name of—Smith. Got throwed by his hoss."

Gina Corbett's soft lips smiled faintly. "Howdy, Mister Smith," she said. "I hope you're better now."

Trent's breath went in slowly and softly and then out again. "Thank you, ma'am," he said. "I'm gettin' all right."

She knew him. He could swear to that. Despite the three weeks' beard that covered his face and the star-scar on his jaw and the dyed silver lock, she knew him well enough. He could have sworn it. Yet despite that first deliberate hesitation between the mister and the Smith she gave no further sign of recognition. But she persisted in staying and talking to him, with the Simses finding seats and having the air of hovering anxiously over the range talk.

At last she said, "Has anybody heard anything of that awful outlaw. Silver Trent? He seems to have disappeared. I suppose he's up to some deviltry or other. His men, thank heaven, are in jail in Mexico. The *Rurales* caught them. They've been tried, I hear, and are to be shot in Cala de Polvo next week. Next Saturday, to be exact—just a week from today. Good riddance—"

She rattled on politely, sweetly, while Silver watched her with his nerves taut and his eyes wondering. Didn't she know him, after all?

"Bob Burney came back from El Paso the other day. He says they've got another of those Trent men there—an old man

41

named Magpie Myers. He's to be tried for murder and the trial's been set for just two weeks from today. Everybody says he's sure to be convicted. An old man like that ought to know better than to be running with cow-thieves and such."

She smiled ravishingly at Silver Trent and then got to her feet. "I'm mighty glad to have met you, Mr. Smith," she said politely. "I hope you're better soon."

Trent stared after her as she took her leave of Joe and Martha Sims.

When old Joe Sims came back they stared at one another, and then Sims shook his head, shrugging. "I'll never git old enough to understand anything about a woman."

"You're an old fool, Joe Sims," his wife said calmly, "but you ain't that big a fool. Go an' git me some wood for the fire."

That was the best Trent ever got out of either of them.

The next day, he got up, dressed, and insisted on having his horse.

"But, hell, Silver," Joe Sims protested. "You're loco. There ain't no hurry. An' you ain't fit to ride yet."

Trent shook his head. "I'm plumb obliged to you, Joe. But I'll be goin' along now."

He buckled on his guns with fumbling fingers, his mouth tight with the effort. And walked out toward the corral.

A saddled horse stood there—a long-legged, deep-chested bay—not the horse he had taken from the *Rurale*. At his questioning look, Joe Sims, said with embarrassment, "He's the best on the place. Take him for at long as you need him."

Trent climbed into the saddle, saying nothing because there was an unexpected tightness in his throat.

As he rode, some of the weakness left him, so that he was pretty sure that he would make out all right. It would take three or four days to ride to Cala, and he'd be gaining strength all the while from now on.

At first it took all his concentration merely to stay in the saddle and to make camp and eat. But as his strength came back, he began to think. It occurred to him that he might have gotten out of Sims' place just in time.

HE HAD taken Gina Corbett's visit to mean one of two things: Either she hadn't recognized him and was just talking, or else she had recognized him and for some unexplainable reason had wanted to tip him off to the situation of his own men. Now, belatedly, it occurred to him that she had been a spy, to find him out and trap him.

How could Gina Corbett be anything but an enemy? She must know something of her father's business. Moreover, she had been there when he had threatened to kill her father and when he actually had slung lead into two of their men. He had learned from Joe Sims that when he had shot the gun out of the hand of the man in the window, the bullet had glanced off and lodged against the man's collarbone, breaking it. The other man, he knew, he had shot in the shoulder. Neither had died, but there was no reason for Gina Corbett to know that he had not meant to kill either of them.

What other purpose could the girl have had in coming to the Sims'—except to trap him? No doubt something had gone wrong. Not enough men had been immediately available for a posse, or else they thought they'd had plenty of time.

And then another idea hit him like a stinging hornet. Maybe that whole talk about his men in Cala had been a trap. Maybe they weren't there. Or if they were, the idea had been to use them as bait, so that when he tried to rescue them they'd be waiting for him....

That tied in completely with all Corbett's past behavior. It had been Corbett, surely, who had set the first trap for him outside Cala de Polvo. And it had been Corbett, almost certainly, who had set the *Rurales* on him at the river. So it would be typical of Corbett to set this trip for him also.

THE WHOLE thing settled into place now in Trent's mind, and with it an overwhelming sense of humiliation at the fool he had been. Corbett had done him out of ten thousand dollars and then had tried to have him killed because he had thought that Silver would guess what had happened. And then luck and Silver's dumbness had conspired to help him again. Clay had made the deal for the second bunch of cattle, and Corbett had struck for the second ten thousand. That had failed, and Silver had come to kill him.

He couldn't fool any longer. Every day that Silver lived was a risk to Corbett. So he had set still another trap, using Silver's own men as bait!

Trent understood now Peirez' laughter that day in jail. Peirez was in this with Corbett, of course. He was being paid, and paid well, for Trent's death!

So Silver Trent's thoughts ran that night as he rolled into his blankets and all at once, unreasonably, it seemed to him that the bottom had dropped out of his world. Yet treachery was no new thing to him.

But Al Corbett hadn't looked like that kind of man. He seized on that thought, as though it explained everything—as though it explained the whole depth of his disappointment. Because Al Corbett had looked like a decent man.

He didn't admit to himself that it meant anything special to him that Gina Corbett should be as bad or worse than her father. He didn't admit that....

That night and the next day were as bad as he had ever known. He rode, under the weight of the next day's sun, with a haunting sense of loneliness and failure. As far as he could see, no creature lived in this desolate land of heat-blasted rock and cactus.

He was alone, and confronted by impossible tasks. His men were gone scattered, marked for death.

Lars and Jim... In jail, waiting death, because they had served Silver Trent—believed in him. And Magpie, also.

He stiffened abruptly in the middle, and then after a moment he lifted his fist and shook it at the pale and burning sky.

"So I'm alone, am I? he snarled. "Well, by God, while I'm alive...."

CHAPTER 6
INTO THE DEATH-TRAP

T HREE DAYS later his bare feet padded softly on dust. The frayed cotton pants that covered his legs were too tight, so that they showed the powerful muscles of his legs. Under the blanket that covered his shoulders and fell in long folds over his body, the sixguns rubbed gently against his upper ribs. The big, peaked, straw sombrero shadowed a face sun-browned enough to pass as Mexican and hid the tell-tale gray of eyes that might have betrayed him.

He kept to the shadows because his bulk and height were too great for a Mexican. And because he knew that there was no man in this town who was not his enemy.

He had spent a day trying to get information among the people of the countryside who were his friends, but he had gotten little enough. He had verified, simply, the fact that Lars and Jim were in the Cala jail. And there was a rumor that there were being held there as a bait for him. It was the common opinion that he would come for them—and die.

The thing looked hopeless enough. The jail would be guarded by Peirez *soldados.* There weren't many of them—only a hundred or so.

He fingered the key in his pocket—the key that Carmencita had given him. Were Jim and Lars in the cell he had been in? Would that key fit other cells?

At thought of Carmencita, his mouth was a grin under the shadow of his sombrero. Why couldn't he love a girl like that?

A dancing girl—a woman without virtue—yet she had helped him at the risk of her life. Whereas the girls of his own race, the magnolia-faced ones who moved with the swiftly innocent grace of young deer—they betrayed him to his enemies....

He moved out of the alley which paralleled the plaza, sliding into the passageway between two buildings. The jail was not on the plaza but on the main street—the Calle de Santiago de Compostello—which led into it and through it.

His movement brought him alongside of a building which he realized suddenly was the *Commandancia.* Yellow light made a narrow frame around a drawn shade.

He paused in the shadow, stooping to get a look under the small space which was between the shade and the window-sill. The opening gave him a full view of the room, and what he saw sent the breath into his lungs in a sharp inhalation. For what he saw was *El Coronel* Ernesto Peirez, *commandante y alcale,* and—Gina Corbett!

SICKNESS SWEPT through him, followed by a red and savage anger. So he had been right! They had sent this girl to lead him into the trap—and she had let herself be used.

The girl was talking. He could hear the tense, passionate tones of her voice without hearing the words. And he could see Peirez laugh at her unpleasantly. And then the Mexican came around from behind his desk, his fleshy hands reaching out for the girl.

Trent saw Gina Corbett shrink back, quick pallor on her cheeks. And then Peirez' greedy hands caught her, jerked her to him. She screamed, fighting away from him. He lifted one hand and slapped her, so that her head bobbled and she was obviously dazed. Then he pulled her violently against his chest and glued his lips to hers.

Blind instinct moved Trent, sent his legs driving toward the front of the building. Yet at the corner of the passageway, he checked. This girl was nothing to him. She had made this situation for herself, by her treachery....

Maybe he could throttle some truth out of this damn sidewinder of a *commandante*. It was all the excuse he needed.

He rounded the corner of the building swiftly, reached the door in two savage strides. A *solado* on guard there gasped a low, startled squawk and tried to get his rifle up. Trent's fist exploded under his jaw, slamming the back of his head against the door jamb, so that he crumpled like a rag-doll.

He went in fast through the darkened corridor and whipped open the unlocked door to Peirez' office.

Gina Corbett had ceased to cry out. She had gotten her hands loose and was clawing desperately at Peirez's face. The Mexican cursed and gave back a little and then his staring eyes whipped to the open door.

He released the girl with a sudden gasp and stepped back, his hand going instinctively to the gun at his belt.

Trent laughed suddenly, savagely.

"Go ahead and fill your hand, Peirez."

Peirez' hand froze as though some blasting paralysis had struck it.

"You?" he breathed. "Trent!"

Trent's hand slid under the *serape* and came out weighted by a gun. "*Sí señor,*" he said with a sudden ferocious gentleness. "And I think now we will have a little talk."

"I—I—" the Mexican stammered, his face the color of a sheet followed by age and filth. "I had to obey the law. I—"

"I'm not interested in your lies, Peirez," Trent said. "I got another use for you."

It had occurred to him suddenly that luck had brought him into exactly the right place. If he had planned it, this couldn't be better.

He kept his eyes steadily away from the girl, but in the fringe of his vision he could see her—still panting, her face pale, but with a thankfulness which was near to fainting in her eyes.

"We'll go to the door, Peirez, and you'll call the sergeant at the jail and tell him to take all his men to the east end of the town. You'll tell him that you got word that Silver Trent would be coming in to try to spring his men and that you want him ambushed before he even thinks there's any danger. Make it good, *hombre.* Don't let anything funny creep into your voice or your eyes. I'll be right in the corridor behind you, and if I get a little notion that you might he tryin' to pull anythin', I'll blow the backbone out of you. So make it good, *amigo,* because I'm achin' to kill you anyway."

Peirez rolled glassy eyes about the room, and then he said, shakily, "*Sí, sí!* will do as you say. I—"

Silver said brusquely to the girl, "You'll come to the doorway, where I can see you. If anything happens I'll kill Peirez first and then you."

She said, "Please, I—I—Yes, I'll do as you say."

At the front door the *commandante* stumbled a little over the still-unconscious guard and then called out sharply, "*Sargento!*"

A *soldado* relayed the call and a heavy-set familiar figure appeared in the jail door and came hurriedly toward the *commandante*.

Peirez gave him his orders to a staccato tone which barely concealed its shakiness, and the sergeant, after a stunned instant, saluted and wheeled to obey.

A FEW minutes, hurriedly formed squads were on their way to the east edge of town. Silver let his breath out slowly, softly. Then he said, "And now we go to the jail, señor. My gun will be under my *serape* but it will be just as dangerous to you as though the muzzle was in the middle of your back. Señorita, you will come with us and be very natural and smiling."

They walked toward the door of the jail, and Silver's pulses began to pound with the nearness of victory. What had looked so hopeless appeared easy now. In a moment, if nothing went wrong....

A figure came through the darkness towards them—slender, hip-flaunting Carmencita whose walk was as full of insolent invitation as her dancing.

She half-halted at the sight of Silver, her scarlet lips parting. Then she came on as though she had noticed nothing, ignoring them. Only the flashing darkness of her eyes flicked hostility at Gina Corbett's face.

Silver could feel Peirez tauten under his hand and knew that his eyes were straining toward Carmencita, trying to send her a message.

Carmencita said, *"Buena sera, Commandante,"* with superb indifference and passed them.

Perez stayed taut, but Silver guessed that it was from rage now. A feeling of apprehension swept through him Peirez must have been suspicious of the dancing girl since that day he, Silver, escaped from jail. If she did nothing now, Perez would be all the more sure that she had had something to do with that escape.

And Silver knew that she would do nothing. Somehow, he had to get her out of this town, along with Jim and Lars.

They were about to turn in at the door of the jail, when the swift pound of boots sounded in the dust of the street.

Silver said swiftly, "Whatever it is, *hombre*—make it good!" And then let his breath out in a quick sigh of relief—for this was Pancho Clay and his men. Tension followed as quickly. For Clay might he in on this double-crossing, too.

The group came up fast, six riders in all, and slid to a rearing halt at sight of the three before the jail. Silver saw Pancho Clay's eyes widen, as though in sudden fear.

In the same instant, Peirez turned toward him swiftly. "Take care, *amigo*," he muttered, and then his hand slapped Silver's gun aside, his knee coming up in a vicious blow.

Half Silver's attention was centered on Pancho Clay and the blurring rip of his hands to his guns. Peirez' movement caught him off-guard and the quick and savage blow to his loins doubled him up.

It saved his life, also, for that moment, Peirez, squawking like a scared chicken, plunged sidewise to the dirt of the street. In the same instant, Pancho Clay's right gun hammered, blasting the night silence into howling shards. Silver felt the hot breath of the bullet on his neck.

His left arm swept out, slapping Gina Corbett back into the door of the jail, while his right brought his gun blasting toward Pancho Clay. The shot missed, but sent Clay's hat whirling from his head and the head itself ducking instinctively as his left gun blared, shooting wild.

Silver jumped through the doorway of the jail, slamming the door behind him.

Gina Corbett got to her feet, gasping, "The soldiers will come! You've got to hurry!"

Silver whirled, wordless, toward the cells. His key slid into the lock of the cell where Jim's and Lars' startled figures stood. The lock turned.

"Out!" Silver snapped. "Were surrounded. Guns in the front room. Get busy."

Jim Clane laughed in sudden exultation and came out of the cell like a hawk released, saying, "Old Silver!" as he went past.

Lars Johannson snorted. "A lot of the damn greasers!" he boomed scornfully. "Do nod be so angsious, *amigo*. We will break dere damn necks for dem."

He stalked out into the office and took two six-guns from the wall, tossing them in his great hands contemptuously. "Dese t'ings!" he muttered scornfully "Well, I bane start wid dem."

SILVER LOOKED a little worried. Lars was mad, and that was far from being good. No telling what he would do or how to keep him in hand. The man had a congenital disbelief in the power of lead as applied to his own enormous body. Bullets! He brushed the idea aside as though he had been talking about flies. And when, finally, he lost his enormous good natured patience, he was apt to forget about his guns and go after his enemies with his bare hands.

It would not do in this situation.

"Come out of it, Lars!" Silver snapped, his voice burring like the hum of a vibrating steel whip. "This is a jackpot—an' I'm still runnin' things."

Lars turned the high-colored broadness of his cheeks and the blazing blue of his eyes toward him. They had the roundness and the flare of lion's eyes, and for one instant it looked as though he would mutiny. Then the great shoulders drooped.

"Hal', Silver, I do w'at you say. You know it."

A bullet ripped through the flimsy door. Another smashed the pane of a window.

"Try the back," Silver said quickly, dashed for the corridor. Lead howling through the side door at the rear met him, snarling past him like a half-exhausted bee. Another gun spoke there, and lead ripped through the door and ricocheted screaming along the adobe of the walls.

"Back!"

As useless to try that door as the front one. Yet they had to do something fast. Before many minutes the soldiers would be back from the edge of town, attracted by the firing. If only there weren't this girl!

Even in his irritation and haste, he wondered why he didn't detest her as she should be detested. Well, anyway, he could leave her to her friends.

"Get down under that desk," he snarled at her. "We're goin' out of here."

There were only four or five men in front. It was a bad chance, because every gun was trained on that door. Somebody, maybe all of them, would be lost on the way out. God knew how many citizens with guns Peirez had managed to muster. But there could be no waiting for the soldiers. That would be straight death.

The girl's voice came to him desperately. "You can't! You can't leave me here with these beasts. Not if you're a man! I'm coming with you. Give me a gun. I can shoot."

She did not wait but sprang to the wall where a Winchester hung, as lead howled through the door and the window.

Silver jumped for the lamp, smashed it, leaving the room in darkness. "We can't go out of here with her," he panted. His mind raced, seeking some trick, some possibility.

He jumped toward the broken window, looking out, his pistol blasting toward the bright flash of an exploding flaming muzzle.

In a doorway down the street a quick figure appeared, flaunting even in that moment. "Silver!" Carmencita's voice cried. "The roofs! There's a trap door."

Pancho Clay's figure whirled out of shadow. His gun blasted. The dancing girl's voice broke off. She groaned, her willowy figure melting in a movement which, even in that moment, was seductive. And then she went down, sobbing.

Trent cursed, his voice thick, blind anger raging through his veins. He jumped for the door.

Jim Clane, who had not seen, cried, "No, Silver!"

But Silver never paused. He flung the door open, and went out—a blasting six-gun in each hand.

It was suicide, so unexpected and so deadly savage that it defeated itself.

FROM THE shadow of his doorway, Pancho Clay screamed and went down. A man at his right coughed wetly and hit the dust, making a retching sound. Gun-thunder and the howl of lead was a hell in that street. Behind Silver, Colt fire beat a death's tattoo, where Jim Clane and Lars slammed into action behind him.

Hell, howling and dying…. Until two men came whipping about the corner of the jail—men who had been shooting at the side door and were too enthusiastic about the success of their side. They died there, lead ripping through them, and the sharp, vicious crack of the Winchester held by the girl helping that lead.

And all at once there was silence. Silence except for the sobbing breath of those who had been hit.

Silver strode swiftly where Carmencita lay breathing sibilantly through teeth clenched against pain.

Silver called her name hoarsely, and her agonized face lifted, the proud, voluptuous lips a grimace of pain.

"Silver," she said in suppressed agony, "why—why wouldn't you look at me?"

She smiled at him suddenly, ravishingly. "You—you were never like the others. You—you are proud and—sweet—like the far hills. I was a fool—but oh, Silver! I—even I—could have been good for you."

Her throat filled, bubbling. "Clay—" she got out thickly. "Clay. No—good. With Peirez, Clay...."

Her head fell back, and the last breath rushbed out of her. Sliver cursed deep in his throat and got up, turning blindly away.

Jim Clane touched his arm. "Look, old timer. We've got to get away—"

But Silver shook his head grimly. There was still something he had to do. He walked toward where Pancho Clay lay groaning. A look told him. Clay had been shot through the stomach. He would die long and in agony, but he would die....

"So it was you," Silver looked down into the man's straining eyes. "You crossed me—with Peirez."

Clay's voice came hoarse, hating, "You—dull-headed—fool! I—own both ranches. You—thought I was Corbett's—agent. Corbett's only—the manager of my Texas ranch. I—I made a mistake. How could I know you—were crazy with luck. Damn you, I've tried to—get you—three times now...."

"Three?" Silver's voice came dully, half-incurious.

Clay's broken laugh racked him from head to foot. "I meant to frame—you—for murder. An' your—fool, Magpie Myers got thee—instead."

Trent snarled, his eyes narrowed and suddenly deadly. "You—"

Clay cackled feebly, "Go ahead, you fool, shoot. Do you think I want this—pain." His dark, half breed face contorted in a snarl of agony.

Beside him a Mexican stirred groaning at the wound that welled redly from his side.

Jim Clane took Silver urgently by the arm "Look, Silver,

they're coming. Are you goin' to fight the whole damn Mexican army."

Silver shook him off and turned to the Mexican. "You were Clay's man," he snarled "What do you know about Magpie Myers. Talk! You're not dead yet, but you can be any minute."

The man gasped. "I was there, señor. It was Señor Clay who killed the man. I will swear it. I-Esteban—had nothing to do with it."

Beside Silver, Gina Corbett's breath drew in deeply.

Suddenly, her soft words came in a tumbling, urgent stream, "Silver, dad didn't know anything about this. Oh, I swear it. He went in with Clay, became his Texas manager because our ranch was about to be lost—but only to receive wet cattle from Mexico He knew nothing of all this. He was so—stunned—when you came there that night."

Silver raised upright, looking suddenly deep into her eyes.

"No," she said desperately. "Don't look at me like that. We didn't know. When you came that night, I thought you were only an outlaw. But, but I saw that you wouldn't shoot dad because he didn't have a gun, and I saw that you shot Mike's gun out of his hand and hit Bill in the shoulder, and I knew you weren't bad. And dad and I both wondered about what you said. And then I found you at Joe Sims' place and—and I told you about your men."

She paused, her breath going in deeply, lifting her soft breasts. "Then when I got home—Clay was there. I heard him talking with dad—boasting that he had you now, wherever you were, because he was holding your two men here in jail, and would hold them as bait until you showed up to get them. And then he and Peirez would get you. I knew that, unintentionally, I had sent you into a trap. So—so I rode after you—to try to cut you off here. And—and—I guess you know the rest."

Jim Clane was plucking at Silver's shoulder. "Look, boy—they're coming."

And they were, in a soft-footed, deadly rush down the street, with Peirez vengeful, snarling face to lead them.

But Silver Trent laughed, because now things were straightened out. What did a lot of Mexicans matter now? "Horses," he barked. "Any horses, *amigos!*"

And then his sixgun mingled its harsh, deep note with the snarling chatter of the *soldados'* rifles.

El Coronel Ernesto Peirez, *commandante y alcalde del Ciudad de Cola de Polvo,* stopped short in his tracks, put a hand to his heart like a man bowing, and fell on his face.

"*Vamonos!*" yelled Silver Trent exultantly. "I think that we'll have old Magpie with us soon. And maybe a ranch or so, too!"

Jim Clane laughed. "*Vamonos* for now! Maybe we'll be back again."

But Lars Johanssen bellowed disgustedly, "Why we ron? Dis is no'ting but greasers."

That was when Silver was in the saddle, with the soft feel of Gina Corbett against his left arm and chest, and his right hand blasting a sixgun warning for *soldados* who hurriedly sought shelter in the shadows.

And after that there were only the high stars wheeling overhead and the beat of hoofs over a land no longer lonely....

THE LAW OF SILVER TRENT

"**IF THIS** state thinks its doin' me any favor," Trent rasped, narrow-eyed, "it's plenty in error."

Across from him, Zeke Burch, captain of Rangers, glared, hunching his blocky, powerful shoulders.

"If that's the way you feel about it," he flared, "why—"

Bill Lang's steady voice cut him off. "Let's everybody take it easy. "Silver figgers he didn't do nothin' to be outlawed for in the first place."

Trent leaned back in his chair, pushing his Stetson back with a characteristic gesture at once casual and impatient. The movement revealed the silver gray lock of hair that ran diagonally up from the peak of his forehead and which had given him his nickname.

His cold gray eyes flicked to Lang and warmed a little. There was something in this quiet, lean man that forced his respect. He remembered a night in Eagle Pass when he and Lang had tangled on opposite sides of the fence. A tough, fast man with his fists, this Ranger sergeant, and chained lightning with a sixgun. If the men with him had been as good, the Trent gang would have been taken that night.

It came to him that Lang and Burch ought to change places. Lang had brains as well as toughness, while the captain had only toughness, and a mind as narrow as a rock tunnel.

Lead smashed at Jim and his horse
like a gust of envenomed sleet....

At that, he didn't quite know why he, Silver Trent, was throwing his bristles around. It wasn't any insult to be pardoned by the governor of Texas and offered a place with the Rangers....

Insult? He drew a deep breath softly. Nobody but himself would ever rightly know just how much this meant to him. After ten years of outlawry, of watching his back trail like a cattle-butchering varmint, and of being fair game for lawman or renegade murderer. And now, to be able to walk the streets of his own land without fear! Sit at a table without being careful to put his back to the wall....

Maybe that was why his nerves were on edge—because this thing meant so much to him. Or maybe it was because of Knife

Trebizo, there at the bar. El Diablo's man, was Knife. The curve of his back, leaning with elbow on the wood was like the sinuous curve of a rattler.

All Trent's instincts yelled "trap" at him, because of Trebizo's presence, and because he had glimpsed Limpy Sim Tolliver disappearing fast into an alley as he had ridden into this town.

Or it might have been the consciousness of Jim Clane, and Pablo, and big Lars Johanssen, waiting there on the other side of the Rio, for this thing to be finally settled.

He remembered them riding with him, Pablo singing some damn hymn by way of proving his lightness of heart, and Lars with a fixed grin that might have fooled a half-wit, and Jim Clane, poker-faced except for the expressions of suspicion and indignation and sheer desolate sorrow that rippled across his pugnacious features.

Knowing how they felt had been hard to bear. But it was for their sake also. If he made good, with a Ranger's commission in his pocket, and could then put in a word for them....

Jim had known it, or had made shift to believe it. Silver remembered Pablo scowling down at the town from the ridge across the river and growling in Spanish, "I don't like the look of this hole of Hell. It has the smell of a trap."

Jim Clane had snarled at him instantly, his voice freighted with the anger of a man fighting himself. "Shut up, you greaser buzzard. Goddlemighty! Cain't you give Silver his chanct without howlin' grief about it? It's our chanct too, if you had sense enough in that dumb spick head to see it."

Now Silver became aware of the silence of the man across

the table from him there, waiting for him to speak. He leaned across the table toward them, his gray eyes level. "I wasn't meanin' to get hostile," he said quietly. "If you're still of the same mind, why I'll say ye—"

The slamming echo of the shot cut him off.

Pure reflex whipped his hands to his guns, had them half way out of leather before the first snarling report, slapping against the adobe walls had faded.

Other shots, two in a pair and then another followed instantly. But by that time, Silver's guns were back in their holsters. The split second had given him time to realize that this probably had nothing to do with him. His men were safe on the Mexican side of the River, and he himself was on safe conduct here. Zeke Burch and Bill Lang, in their separate ways, were square men.

Yet his eye flicked to Knife Trebizo and the other Mexican there at the bar, the gray of his gaze flat and cold, and the set of his big shoulders like that of a cat waiting on a game trail.

The two Rangers had slapped to their feet, were moving toward the bar door.

"Jefe! Jefe! Watch yourself. They have Jeem an' Lars!" The cry came from outside, choked, panting. Pablo's voice!

Silver cursed under his breath and hit the doorway so fast that he had to knock Burch and Lang out of his way.

His guns were out, but the street that met his gaze was deserted except for Pablo, leaning, half-falling against an adobe opposite, the side of his silk shirt stained darkly.

"What happened? Quick!"

The lean face of the Mexican shook impatiently at the question. "Jeem—Lars," he panted. "They got them—took them away. El Diablo—"

Silver cursed, whirled on the two Rangers. His eyes slapped at them with the force of a physical blow.

"If you had anything to do with this, damn you," he snarled, "I'll—"

Bill Lang's troubled eyes met his unflinchingly. "Not a thing, Silver. I'll give you my word on it."

"Get to the ford then," Trent ripped out. "We've got to cut them off."

The last words were called over his shoulder as he ran.

This Border town of Roadrunner was no more than a straggle of adobes along a single street paralleling the river. The cantina in which Silver had met the Rangers was near the end of the town which ran down toward the ford. The shooting had come from the opposite direction. But if it were El Diablo's men who had done this, Jim and Lars would be taken back to Mexico. Therefore, they'd have to cross the ford. And that gave Silver the jump on them. If he hurried, he could cut them off.

These thoughts raced through his mind in the moments it took his long, pistoning legs to hit the end of the street and turn toward the river.

He brought up suddenly, puzzled. The ford was empty. The brown waters swirled in sluggish serenity under the down stroke of the sun. The metallic-rocky hills beyond lay glinted bare and silent. The near bank was deserted.

And then, all at once, from the far side of town, hoof beats sounded, going fast, then fading.

Silver whirled on the two lawmen behind him, narrow-eyed. "What's goin' on here?" His voice was a slap; hard, suspicious.

Hot-eyed, Zeke Burch glared back at him. "Damn you—"

But Silver's harsh voice cut him off. "Ever hear of Don Esteban Bautista y Varro—sometimes known as El Diablo?" he asked softly.

Zeke Burch looked honestly puzzled. "Why—yeah. Some kind of big auger down below the Border, ain't he? I—"

"Did I hear somebody mention my name?" The voice came from Silver's left, clear, gently modulated, mocking.

Silver drew a long soft breath and turned slowly. "Speak of the devil!" he said grimly.

THE MAN who stood there in the hot sunlight was dressed in black. He had been dressed in black the last time Silver had seen him. Only that time, the clothes had been Mexican, and a long cloak had sheathed the misshapen blotch of his twisted body. Now, the clothes were such as a prosperous Texas rancher might wear, and the result was somehow more grotesque and sinister. One shoulder hunched up, one arm looked somehow foreshortened and withered, so that the long, beak-nosed face under the black Stetson made up the general appearance of a buzzard half asleep in the sun. Only the piercing life of the black eyes and the cruel intelligence of the thin mouth belied that appearance.

Out of the corner of his eye, Silver saw that the two Rangers were staring at this figure with open bewilderment, and he knew all at once that they had nothing to do with the thing which had happened.

His right hand tightened about the six-gun which he still carried unsheathed, the heat of his hatred coming up red behind his eyes. He still didn't know exactly what had happened, but he did know that this thing before him was more viciously evil than any gila monster that ever flicked a tongue in the sunlight, and that its presence was overdue in hell.

"This is the state boundary-line," Burch said flatly. "It's as far as we go."

"I think you've maybe made a mistake, Varro," he said thickly. "What are you doin' to my men?"

The lean, misshapen figure before him showed polite surprise. "My dear friend," he protested, "what have I to do with your—

unfortunate followers?" He put a sardonic emphasis on the last words.

Silver's gaze was suddenly cold and wicked. He flicked up the sixgun. "After all," he said gently, "why talk? It's been a long time. Too long."

Bill Lang's voice cut in, smudging out the sudden fear in Varro's eyes. "Easy does it, Silver. Is there anything against this gent?"

Silver said, "Plenty," his eyes narrowed, deadly, so that the color that had come back into Varro's face faded again. "More than I got time to tell you now. For one thing, though, he's responsible for havin' my men taken. Sim Tolliver was in it—and Tolliver's one of his men."

That was a shot in the dark, but he felt certain enough of himself.

"Can you prove that?" Varro sneered, but the fear was still there.

And then, all at once, he got hold of himself. "Captain," he said, deferentially, addressing Burch, "I happened to overhear someone say that those two men—Clane was it, and Johanssen?—are wanted badly for a hanging in New Mexico. Maybe the men who—er—took them, are deputies from that territory."

The full force of that hit Silver like a landslide. Jim and Lars *were* wanted in New Mexico, for a murder that they hadn't done. But that last couldn't be proved. And this Texas town of Roadrunner was in the angle formed by Mexico, Texas and New Mexico—not thirty miles from the new Mexican line.

Once they were across that line....

He cursed savagely, aloud. Varro had engineered this. He was responsible. Nobody else could be. His men were carrying Jim and Lars into New Mexico, where they would be met by New Mexican lawmen, fixed by Varro, and arrested!

He whipped up the barrel of his gun again, "By God, Varro," he snarled, "I've had enough of givin' you a man's chance! You've murdered and double-crossed and schemed and destroyed, so that you ought to have been in hell these last ten years. You can try to yank a gun. I'm putting mine in leather. But I'm pullin' again right away. Drag iron, you hydrophobia skunk—because you're dyin' now!"

New panic blanched Varro's face as Silver's gun slid into its holster, his big hand hovering over it to draw again.

"Captain!" he squawked, "this *hombre* is mad—loco! I've done nothing. Are you going to stand there and let him kill me?"

Zeke Burch's gun was suddenly in Silver's ribs. "No, I'm not lettin' him kill you," he said grimly. "Though I ain't far from figgerin' that you need it. Take it easy, Trent. It's the law talkin'."

Silver drew a long slow breath and then let his hand fall away from his gun.

"All right, Burch," he said grimly, "but I'm goin' after my men. If you want to try stoppin' me, we'll see if you can shoot me before I take that iron an' shove it down your throat."

Zeke Burch grunted, glaring. "We're goin' after 'em all right," he said sourly. "Nobody's goin' to pull anythin' like this under my nose an' get away with it."

Silver turned, moving toward the street, with the uneasy feeling that this devil Varro had somewhat tricked him again.

And moving so, he wondered all at once whether that was not one reason for his complete hatred of the man. Nobody else had ever shown that he could out-think Silver Trent. Yet this man had shown it more than once, and now had shown it once again. He had been playing for time—time for his men to get away with Jim and Lars. And he had counted on the Rangers to keep Silver from killing him!

CHAPTER 2
HELL'S HOSTAGES

PABLO WAS flat on his back in the saloon, with the fat gray-haired bartender bending over him. His eyes were closed, his face gray.

The bartender adjusted the final loop of a bandage. "Hit in the side," he grunted. "Cracked a couple of ribs but dee-flected around an' out. He'll live. Only needs a couple of weeks' rest."

Pablo sat up suddenly. *"Jefe!"* he said painfully. "We must ride. Jeem an'—"

"I'm ridin', old timer," Silver said gently. "Me an' these other gents. You stay here."

"No!" Pablo's negation was violent.

Silver's eyes hardened. "You heard my order, *hombre,*" he said coldly.

Pablo lay back, feebly. *"Sí, Jefe,"* he murmured. "I have heard."

Silver's eyes warmed. "So long, *amigo.*" Then he turned a hard gaze on the bartender. "See that he's all right an' you won't lose by it. But if anything happens to him, I'll be askin' you why."

69

They were ten miles out along the trail before Pablo caught up with them.

Silver cursed him in Spanish, including his ancestors for a long way back.

"*Jefe,*" Pablo said grimly, "It is not well to blaspheme." His lean, ascetic face was gray, but calm and unmoved.

"I told you to stay," Silver snarled.

Pablo shrugged. "This little hurt is nothing. Pouf! The bite of a fly."

He spurred his horse up alongside and murmured, "Besides, these animals are of the law. What if you needed somebody in a tight place?"

Silver glowered a deep irritation running in him. That was a hell of a thing for Pablo to say to him, when he, Silver, was also of the law now—or practically so! But his anger was mostly at himself, because he caught himself feeling what Pablo felt—sensed that somehow, inside him, he was still on the wrong side of the fence, still somehow distrustful of these Rangers who were to be his riding mates from now on.

He turned a bleak gaze on Pablo. "Somethin' the matter with bein' on the side of the law?" he demanded aggressively.

Pablo looked abashed. "N-no," he murmured. "Only...."

"Ferget all that," Silver advised him harshly. "Now—what happened?"

"We—we got uneasy—up there on the hill." The lean Mexican's speech was short-clipped, as a man speaks when it is difficult for him to speak at all. The gray pallor of his face sent a pang through Silver, thrusting his anger away. "Through the long glasses we saw Limpy Sim Tolliver and also a glimpse of someone who might have been El Diablo. Such sights are not good for the soul. And there was the sense in me, *Jefe*, that this place was a trap. We rode in.

"I stopped to talk to a girl, *Jefe*. Through the window we could hear her berating her lover in terms that were not just— merely because he had made love to her! This is not—pleasing to heaven, *amigo.*"

Silver looked at him, the remnant of his anger slipping away in a half smile. "You condone sin, Pablo?" he demanded.

"There is no sin where there is love, *Jefe*," Pablo said.

"Love for the sinner or love for the sin?" Silver asked wickedly.

Pablo shrugged, and grimaced with the pain of that. But he said calmly. "Sin or sinner, what does it matter, *Jefe?* It is love which is acceptable to the saints. It was that which I told to this *chiquita.*"

"And—?"

"Lars and Jeem had gone on ahead. A *hombre* that we knew— Spleetleep Flane—he sticks a gun in Jeem's back from a doorway that opens fast. But Buck Trury hits Lars behind the ear—a blow to kill a longhorn. I think he knows that Lars does not believe in bullets and will not stay still with a gun in his back, so he knocks him out, pronto. But Jeem is smart. He stands still. Like I would do."

"And then?"

"My gun is very fast, *amigo*, but not fast enough for Leempy Tolliver, who is in the alleyway where I do not see him. The bullet hits me and I am all of a sudden very weak. I do not know just

71

what goes on. I shoot, twice, but I miss. Then somebody shoots at me as I drop. I am still, I cannot make my gun-hand move. They take Lars and Jeem and put them on horses and then they are away, but I get up then and shoot some more, but no use. Then I run an' yell for you."

Silver said, narrow-eyed, "Splitlip Flane and Buck Trury and Limpy Tolliver. They're all El Diablo's hands, but who can prove it?" He swore under his breath.

THE RANGER captain, Zeke Burch, pulled up suddenly. "Where we goin' now?" he rasped. "This trail has run out."

Silver looked at him with eyes widened by surprise.

The trail was clear. A child could have followed it. At least, that was what Magpie Myers would have said. Magpie pretended profound contempt for Silver's trailing ability, having been, to a large extent, Silver's teacher.

The point was that though these Texas Rangers were good men and better than average trackers, they still didn't have the training of men like Silver and Pablo.

"I think we'll catch a trace or so later on," he said quietly, and took the lead.

The trail was not only clear to such eyes as his own, but it was freshening. Silver guessed that his quarry was not more than a quarter of a mile ahead.

But the New Mexican Border was not far ahead, either.

He spurred on, stepping up the pace. Thank God these lawmen were well mounted, at least. The whole thing hinged, he knew, on whether they could catch up with El Diablo's men before they got into New Mexico. Or, if they missed that, on whether the New Mexican lawmen were waiting just over the line.

He whipped his horse around a bend in the rocky trail, saw the stirred rock of a downslide and put the animal to the slope with a flick of his reins and a swift movement of his legs. The big sorrel jumped from the ledge like a diver taking off, hit loose rock and slide, legs bunched as Silver leaned far back in the saddle.

The trail ran straight toward a new trail at the bottom, but it was a trail flanked by abysses. If the horse got turned sideways, he would roll, and, rolling, miss that narrow way, to go tumbling down the side of a sheer drop.

Silver had taken that way without a thought, with hardly a quickening heat of his pulse, until, when he was half way down the slide, he thought of Pablo. Pablo, gray-faced, and already rocking in the saddle from loss of blood…. Could Pablo do this?

But his fear had been needless. Pablo, calm-eyed, was already down, just behind him, and Zeke Burch was just finishing the downward slide. Only, Burch's face was white and sweating.

Behind Burch, Bill Lang hit the slope, poker-faced, and slid into the clear. Silver knew then that between Burch and Lang there was no trouble of choice. Bill Lang was the better man by far.

But what hit him the hardest was the thought, again, that no one of his men would have turned gray over such a slide, that somehow he was tied up with men who were not as tough. For Bill Lang had been wooden-faced, yet the mask of his face was stiff, and Silver knew that under it was fear.

The twisting course of the canyon led him abruptly onto a ledge which brought his horse to a sliding stop. The trail led along the ledge to the left and then down, but from where he had stopped he could see across the floor of a flat valley, and on the valley floor, not three hundred yards away, were the men he sought.

There were five horses. Two of them bore Jim Clane and Lars Johanssen, bound in the saddle. And the other three were Buck Trury and Limpy Tolliver and Splitlip Flane. In that clear air, it was easy to make them out.

Silver's hand whipped instinctively to the Winchester in his saddle boot, then checked. At three hundred yards he might miss, but whether he did or not, there would still be two men left to kill Lars and Jim. He did not dare shoot.

He swung his horse to the left, riding down from the ledge. As he rode he saw, with a sudden tightening of his jaw, a single stone marker which he knew showed the boundary between Texas and New Mexico.

His eye searched the tangle of badlands beyond for a glimpse of New Mexican lawmen, but nothing stirred there. There was still a chance. They were four to three now, and if they rode boldly up the El Diablo men would have to give in, even though they held Lars and Jim as shields.

He knew that kind of cattle. They'd bluff about killing Lars and Jim if anybody came closer, but it would be only bluff. Confronted with four determined men, they would never have the nerve to kill either of the prisoners, for that would be murder under the very eyes of the law. More than that, it would be....

Silver checked his thought there, because he did not want quite to go through with it. But the thought was clear enough. Not one of these three coyotes would kill a man of Silver's under such circumstances, because they knew in their hearts that no hole would be small enough or far enough to hide them from Silver's vengeance. And the thought of that vengeance would be more powerful than the fear of all the Rangers in Texas.

He drove on, knowing now that the quarry was his. Drove on until his horse's hoofs crossed the boundary marked by that white stone. And then Zeke Burch's voice slapped at him from behind."

"Far enough, Trent. This is where we stop."

SILVER PULLED up and stared at him, only half comprehending. "What are you talking about, *hombre?*"

"This is the state boundary line," Zeke Burch said flatly. "This is as far as we go."

A kind of bitter, unbelieving anger buzzed along Silver's veins. "You mean you won't cross this line, even though there's no law on the other side of it, and even though these men broke the law in Texas?"

"That's right, pardner." Zeke's voice was harsh. "This here's our deadline. An' that includes you."

"Me?" The anger was beginning to get away with Silver, so that his voice had the faint, dangerous undertone of a buzz saw.

"You're a Ranger, ain't you? I thought I heard you say 'yes' back there."

Silver's cold eyes searched him savagely, but before he could find words to answer, Bill Lang cut in. "He hasn't taken the oath yet, Zeke. There's nothin' in the law that says he can't cross into New Mexico."

Silver did not even wait for Burch's answer. He said, "So long, boys," grimly, and turned and rode. Behind him he heard the hoof beats of Pablo's horse.

The crowd ahead disappeared into the mouth of an unwinding arroyo.

Behind Silver, Pablo said exactly nothing—but he might as well have been yelling as far as Silver was concerned. He remembered the old Mexican's whisper, "These animals are of the law, *Jefe*. What if you needed somebody in a tight place?"

But Pablo was not fool enough to say "I told you so" to any man.

And then that thought, too, went out of Silver's mind as he turned his whole mind to the tack ahead. He did not take the arroyo he had seen El Diablo's men enter. He set a course to the left, some instinct for terrain telling him how to climb over and short cut that.

Even so, the vicious whine of a bullet was the first warning he had that they had come up with the men in front. The lead keened across a ridge up which he was picking a cautious way, and it came close, the snarl of it like a passing slap at his ear drum. He hit the ground fast, on the near side of his horse and crawled up fast to the rise of the ground, shoving his Stetson off and raising his head cautiously.

It was as though the lift of his head was a trigger finger, setting off rifle fire. Lead snapped in to the bank before him, set up its high snarl an inch above him.

Yet that glimpse had told him enough.

They were there, in the open. This canyon widened out into a long Vee. They had not meant to be caught there, and their only hope was to keep their pursuers down below this ridge until they could get to the lead-in arroyo that promised cover.

But beyond them was something more important.

Four or five hundred yards away, on the lift of a ridge sat a body of horsemen, motionless. And Silver knew instinctively that this was a New Mexican posse, brought out to collect Lars and Jim, as per the message from one El Diablo.

Savage curses rolled from his taut throat, as, moving like flashing automaton, he whipped sideways and came up with his hands gun-filled. The blue-faded muzzles of the .45's flared pale flame against the sunlight. Long shots. Yet Buck Trury and Splitlip Flane pitched from their saddles as though a giant wind had blown them down.

Limpy Sim Tolliver had his rifle to his shoulder and shot once. But after that he didn't delay. He hit steel to his horse cruelly and jumped toward the arroyo, leading Lars Johanssen's horse.

Beside Silver, Pablo's gun blasted. A split second afterward, Silver's Colts laid their savage impact on the hot air.

Tolliver's racing horse jerked and jumped like a puppet pulled by a string and then disappeared, lumbering heavily into the arroyo.

The animal bearing Lars followed him out of sight. On the ridge beyond, the posse broke into cautious movement, spreading out arid coming slowly down the slope.

Silver swung into the saddle, spurring toward Jim Clane's horse, which was whirling indecisively about in the open, spooked and not knowing which way to run. The pound of racing hoofs toward him decided the animal to take out toward the arroyo up which Limpy and Lars had catapulted.

Silver whirled that way.

CHAPTER 3
INTO HELL'S CORNER

FROM THE slope in front, a Winchester keened its thin, wicked note through the sunblasted air. The bullet hit a rock a hundred yards short of them and ricochetted into space with a faint scream.

Behind Silver, Pablo's rifle snarled in reply. Silver jerked his head rearwards. "Don't!" he yelled through taut lips. And an instant later, he swung into the arroyo.

He was in time to see Lars' big body down on the sandy floor and Limpy Sim, on Lars' horse, disappearing about a bend in the wash. Jim Clane's horse had pulled up, snorting, at the human obstacle in his path, held by long habit and by Jim's soothing, "Whoa! Whoa, boy."

Silver snapped, "Shut it off ahead, Pablo," and Pablo's mount catapulted past him, swerving to miss Lars' body and pulling up to block Jim's horse from escape up the arroyo. But the jug-headed roan Jim rode had suddenly decided to behave. He pawed the sand of the arroyo a moment and then turned, and casually-started to nibble at a mesquite bush that grew on the arroyo's banks. It took ten seconds after that to cut Lars and Jim's bonds.

Lars stood up and began cursing in the direction which Limpy Sim Tolliver had taken. The thickness of his Scandinavian accent was a measure for the anger that had been seething in him.

But Jim Clane, sitting his horse now with his hands on the bridle, said worriedly to Silver, "There's a posse comin'."

Silver's eyes narrowed but he made no answer. Only the hard jut of his jaw as he turned back toward the mouth of the arroyo betrayed his thoughts.

Pablo said quietly, sharply, *"Jefe!"* But Silver did not pause.

At the arroyo's mouth it was possible to see the posse, still nearly two hundred yards away, because Silver's shooting had inspired that much caution.

Fifteen feet away, Splitlip Flane lay groaning. Beyond him, Buck Trury made a limp insensible blot against the rocks of the canyon floor.

Silver disregarded the posse as he pulled up by Flane and dismounted. "Take it easy, *hombre*," he said quietly. "Let me look at that wound of yours."

Flane's wide, broken-nose face twisted into a ghastly venomous mask. "You've killed me, you snake," he rasped. "To hell with you! Wait—until—El Diablo...."

"Where's El Diablo?" Silver asked quickly.

"Waitin' fer yuh at the corner of the Border," Flane gasped. "You're—whip-sawed between the—law an'—the—devil!"

His head lifted in a gasp of agony and then fell back limply.

A thin stream of scarlet gushed from his mouth and then was stilled.

Silver stood up, the corners of his mouth pale, hardly aware of his men who had come up and stood near him.

Beyond, the posse had pulled up warily, rifles held across their saddles, ready to snap to taut shoulders. Less than a hundred and fifty yards away—and dangerous now.

Silver glanced over his shoulder. Across the ridge, on the high ground which was Texas, five riders sat tense and waiting. They were the Rangers—Zeke Burch and Lang, and three others that Zeke had sent word to before they left Roadrunner.

His mind formed a picture of that, made it into a kaleido-scope that took in the New Mexican posse ahead of him and the invisible surety of El Diablo, waiting across the Border for him to come running. It was only then that the full subtlety and completeness of this plan of El Diablo's came to him. A trap which only that humped devil could have conceived.

BACK IN Texas were the Rangers who had invited him to join them, backed by the governor's pardon. But for him only—not for his men. There in Texas these men of his were not wanted murderers, but they were wanted men. They would go to prison as outlaws. Zeke Burch would see to that. Silver knew now the man's temper, his unyieldingness. That was one side. On the other, here in New Mexico, was a posse that wanted them for murder. A posse that would hang them, no doubt, since they were in El Diablo's pay, before a court could convict them.

On the third side was a barrier of cliffs, virtually impassable, but leading inland, anyway, even if they were passed—inland into New Mexico, or Texas and capture.

And on the fourth side was El Diablo and his mixed crew of gun-hung renegades just across the Border, waiting to close the trap with bloody finality.

Pablo's urgent voice broke in on Silver's seething thought. *"Jefe!* You mus' go back. Here is no—"

Jim Clane's clipped tones rapped through. "He's right, Silver. Raise dust toward Texas. The Rangers are waitin' for that. Don't forget—"

It had taken Lars' mind that time to take this in. "Ve take care of dis foolishment, boss. You pull out, like Jim say."

Silver said slowly, "Why, no, boys. I'm in this, too."

Jim Clane turned on him then, his square, tough face flushed at the cheekbones, his blue eyes bleak and uncompromising. "You talk like you're loco," he snarled. "We can get out of this. We ain't exactly wet behind the ears yet. Git over to the Rangers while you still got a chanct to go through with it. You ain't broke no law. They'll take you in an' glad to get you,"

From the slope beyond a voice rang out. "Give up, you *hombres,* or we're ridin' in to take you."

Silver looked at the hunched figure with the long-necked head bobbing On its shoulders, and knew all at once who it was. Buzzard Gates—Sheriff Buzzard Gates—a lawman so crooked that he couldn't have wormed into a castoff sidewinder's skin. And beside him the lean voracious figure of his tentpole deputy, Stretch Lassiter.

"Jefe," Pablo said, with agony on his blood-drained face, "do

not be always a fool. Look! They are waiting for you—everything we have been hoping for. *Jefe!* Name of name of Mary! Go back to them quickly. We will give up to these imbeciles, for a little while, until Charlie and the rest can get us out of jail. And after that—"

"We'd go back with you to take whatever Texas had for us, Silver," Jim Clane said, "but we can't get away from these coyotes now without shootin', an'—an' we don't want to go to shootin' at the law. Not now, when…. Goddlemighty, Silver. Go on! Will yuh?"

Silver stood rigid, knowing that here was his ultimate choice. He had to resist the law or go with it. He had to take the new world that opened to him, or go back to the life of the hunted.

"Reach for sky, you *hombres,*" the voice of Sheriff Buzzard Gates bellowed. "We're movin' in!"

SILVER LOOKED back at the five Rangers sitting their horses there still, with the sense of tension in their motionless figures. Then deliberately he turned toward the oncoming posse, a long pistol shot off now.

Briefly, his eyes rested on his men, then his voice laid its quiet inexorable command on them. "Hit for that arroyo, and fast, *amigos!*" And his hands blurred to his guns, without waiting for their obedience.

"If any jasper thinks he can outshoot Silver Trent, he can fill his hand, and die fast," he sang out grimly. "Watch your hat, Gates."

The guns in his hands made a double report. Nearly a hundred yards away, Buzzard Gates' Stetson jumped from his hat and sailed to the ground with a double hole in its peak.

It was as though a sudden paralysis had hit the whole posse. They did not move or look for cover. They merely sat there, looking slackjawed at the sheriff's hat. And while they sat so, Silver Trent swung his horse and moved toward the arroyo. Grinning suddenly, his men moved with him.

Silver did not move fast. He had known, virtually before he shot, that there would be no need to hurry. This New Mexican posse was made up of ordinary men, brave enough at need, perhaps, but with no stomach to die in a gunfight with outlaws whose reputation was as fighters too well known—and against whom no man in the crowd had a personal grievance. They had been ready enough to ride to collect a couple of wanted men who would be turned over to them, bound and helpless. But this was different.

And so Silver rode into that arroyo which led toward Mexico without haste. But before the arroyo's walls shut off his view, he saw Zeke Burch turn his horse sharply and give a movement of his arm which could mean only one thing—the Rangers would ride parallel to them, on the Texas side, to see that they did not go back into that state.

If they did try, it would be a case of shoot-out with Burch and his men. For not only Silver's men were wanted now, but Silver also. It was easy to read Zeke Burch's mind—like following a narrow way between walls that allowed no straying.

Silver had disobeyed him, to begin with. And to end with, he had fired on an officer of the law. It wouldn't matter to Burch that the lawman had been a vulture, bribed by El Diablo. It would be enough that Silver had gone against the law.

That, exactly, was why Silver had fired the shots that had taken Sheriff Gates' Stetson from his head—to make this thing clear and without the possibility of change.

This he knew, hard-jawed, as they rode down the arroyo that led toward Mexico.

But Jim Clane said irritably, "Silver, yo're a fool. You haven't done nothin' now but put yourself under the devil's hoof."

Silver knew what he meant, and wanted to answer him clearly, but there was a devil of bitterness in him then which made him say, "You mean you're afraid of El Diablo, *amigo?* You think it would have been easier to fight the sheriff's posse, or the Rangers?"

Jim Clane whirled, his eyes flaming, his hands clawing over his guns. "I'm not taking that!" he panted.

Silver's eyes, hard and mocking, held him. Until the red headed man's sullen gaze dropped.

"I'm not the man to be ridden—even by you; don't forget that, Trent," he muttered, staring hard between his horse's ears.

Silver could have stopped that, then and there, with a word, but there was an unreasoning anger in him that withheld him. Maybe the anger was partly because of what he had just sacrificed. Maybe, in part, it was because of his disappointment that the law, as represented by the Texas Rangers was not such as he could follow. Honesty and the respect of his kind he had wanted. But at the cost of letting a friend go to hell, because of an intangible boundary line—a frail fence of red tape?

And on top of all that was Jim's word, "Trent." Not "Silver," but "Trent." He'd make Jim eat that.

Afterwards, he would have given something to eat it himself, but it was to be too late then....

LARS, WHO had caught up Buck Trury's horse and was riding nose to tail with Silver, said, bewildered, "Look, Silver," protestingly.

Silver turned a glacial glance on him and said, "Well?"

A slow flush crept up Lars' great, high-cheek-boned face. "Why—"he mumbled, "I—why—hall! I bane not remember...."

Silver rode on, stony-faced, because this was two things he had to hate himself for. He didn't look at Pablo, because he knew what Pablo's eyes would hold, and he didn't want any part of that.

Instead he looked to his left and saw, through a break in the maze of ravine and wash they had been following, five moving figures five hundred yards away, in Texas. Zeke Burch was grimly paralleling their course.

He laughed at Zeke Burch grimly, and then let his eyes wander back at the other escorting party—the New Mexican posse that paralleled his way, a little behind on the right.

The sight of them ruffed the hairs on the back of his neck. He had half a mind to turn on first one and then the other of them, to find out just how much they had to give out.

In that mood there was no consideration of caution that withheld him. There was only the certainty that El Diablo was ahead, and that beside that game, the law parties were of small consequence.

They crossed the Rio. It was not the boundary here as it was down in Texas. Silver's brooding eyes searched the far banks automatically, knowing that El Diablo would not spoil his own game by shooting on American soil. He would be waiting a little farther on, where the whitewashed boundary posts marked off the difference between interference and murder.

A boundary mark showed, absurdly white against the metallic bare rock.

The trail split here, but there was a third possible way up over a spur of rock, and this Silver took, fast.

A bullet slammed through the late afternoon quiet, the whine and spat of it against rock preceding the thin snarl of the rifle's report. That single shot showed him that his way was right.

He snapped "Ride!" and went over the hump, racing downward, still to the right.

Men swarmed out of the rocks to the left. Lead sung and whined through the air about him. El Diablo had anticipated this possible move, had set this trap.

A goat's trail over an upthrust of rock to the right showed faintly. Once under the shelter of the down spur there would be only a scrambling moment when they would be under fire going up. And then shelter. And then, by the clear lay of the land, escape.

A flicking glance showed him five men on a height of land two hundred yards away to the left, and because this was Zeke Burch and his men, he knew that land was Texas. Behind him, half a mile distant, on a high spur, was Buzzard Gates' crowd in New Mexico. Here was the corner. But he himself was on

Mexican soil now. Behind him was no retreat, and before him was El Diablo.

He wanted to ride straight down and fight it out. But that was madness and suicide for himself and his men.

"Up! After me!" he yelled, putting his winded, laboring mount toward that faint trace of goat hoofs that he might not even have seen, except for the late slanting light of the sun.

He was half way up the first slant, with the lead still howling at him before the full blasting sense of Jim Clane's snarl got through his ears to his racing brain.

"What the hell's the matter with you—afraid of El Diablo?" Jim Clane yelled derisively.

And then Jim's horse was plunging straight down the slope toward El Diablo's guns!

CHAPTER 4
"ONE FOR ALL—
ALL FOR ONE!"

SILVER GROANED and swung his horse in a pivot that would have made a circus rider's fame—the hind hoofs on the slope and the fore hoofs swinging in a great arc to plunge downward again in a perilous scatter of loose rock.

His downward drive barely missed Pablo who was following, his face like the ghost of himself, and even in that moment Silver had a burning pang of conscience because Pablo had no business to be in any fight. But the guilt was in his heart too, because it was his own driving temper which had angered Jim to the madly suicidal thing he was doing now.

He yelled, "Jim! Hit the ground. Take cover."

He doubted if Jim heard him. The brick-haired *halcón*, as Silver's men were called below the Border, was driving straight ahead with both guns hammering a hell's tattoo of challenge at El Diablo's men. They were crouched behind the rocks below and, for a moment, seemed too stunned by this unexpected and utterly reckless charge to fire.

That moment of paralysis cost them two fighting men. One over-eager head reared, lifted-gun ready to knock off this mad gringo, and then, as Jim's deadly gun picked him out, it jerked backward with a spurting hole between the eyes. Another, trying to shift position, took a slug in the shoulder and went down squawling.

Then the answering storm broke. It was as though every man of the score or more there had fired at once. Lead smashed at Jim and his horse like a gust of envenomed sleet. It slammed his horse in a sliding halt, forelegs plowing forward, the animal dead even before he stopped.

And in the same instant, Jim Clane's body shook like a grease-wood branch in a flurry of wind. He swayed in the saddle and hit the ground even before his horse toppled over.

Silver yelled. "Jim!" in an agonized voice. And drove on, toward the prone, crumpled figure on the rocks.

As he rode, during those few seconds, the butts of his guns hammered against his palms. He was shooting with all the cold deadliness which lay in his reflexes, while his mind cursed himself and the men before him.

Behind him he could hear the beat of hoofs on rock and Pablo's guns blaring counterpoint to his own. And Lars Johanssen's savage, cursing yell, like a bellow of bull rage behind him.

He hit the ground beside Jim, slapping his horse aside as he did so, and flung himself down, yelling at the others, "Down! Take cover."

His big hands reached out like steel hooks and dragged Jim's limp body behind the shelter of a rock.

And that way they were trapped.

There wasn't any chance to take the back trail, to go where the goats had gone. Even to get up once from the shelter of these rocks would be to invite certain death. And Silver Trent had the crushing sense that this was his doing, that he had trapped himself and the others.

He had been a self-centered fool, he reflected bitterly. The hurt of shutting himself once more away from the law had put his fool temper up. And so he had insulted Jim to madness—a madness that had trapped not only himself—who deserved it— but Pablo and Lars as well.

They were caught out in the open, with only a scattered barrier of boulders between them and men who would cut them down to dog-meat. To go back was impossible. To charge ahead, with the odds worse than five to one, was suicide. And to stay here, was to be whittled away, until the final shot would find only corpses into which to embed itself.

Silver Trent, outlaw, smart enough and tough enough to

find his way out of half a hundred death traps, had never been in a trap so tight or so deadly. And all because of a moment of temper.

WORSE, HE thought, hammering a lightning slug at a movement in the rocks ahead—much worse! It was because he had fooled with the law. What in hell had he had to do with those hidebound devils, the Rangers? That wasn't the way he fought, tied up in the red tape of the law. His justice was free justice—dealing with the thing itself, whatever it was, in terms of itself.

No. The law was the law, crooked or straight, stupid or right, or hammering blindly ahead to a technical justice. The law was the law—and in its essence, great. But he was Trent—outside the law by no mere accident, but by an inner necessity that demanded a closer, subtler justice. He was a man damned by fate and his own exacting conscience. And he had tried to escape that. Had tried to take the easy, the safe, protected way—to find himself praised by fools and the rabbity folk who crouched, nibbling inside the magic circle of social convention and the predatory coyotes who worked their robberies prudently within the law. That had been his temptation—and he had yielded to it.

To be a badge-toter, a domesticated hunter, brave only when the sterile letter of justice was behind him…!

He snorted with self-contempt. And then he lay with the bitter wonder on him that this ultimate truth about himself should come so clearly only when the shadow of death lay over him, when the only immediate certainty was the final bullet that would rip through him to make the end.

A slug screamed off the rock in front of him, lashing his cheek with brittle splinters. At his side, Jim Clane groaned, muttering. Silver put out exploratory fingers, trying to feel out the bullet wounds that sucked at Jim Clane's life. Maybe, if Jim could be gotten to a doctor....

A glance behind him showed the Rangers on a high point of Texas, looking over this tragic battle. If the fight ended and dying men were left here on Mexican soil, would some Rangers defy regulations and slip down to take what was left of Jim Clane to a medico.

His eyes swung to the others. "Look," he said, "we haven't got a chance here. Suppose we crawl forward, takin' all cover, until we can really get at them. We'll die, but so will most of them. What do you say, *Halcónes?*"

The last word brought a lift of pride into his voice, and he knew what it would do to them. *Halcónes de las Sierras*—Trent's Hawks—who preyed on the rich who oppressed, and helped the poor, and held the balance fair for all honest men! The last fight for them, but that was no great thing, and there were others still to carry on.

His mind flickered to them, back there in the hideout—Magpie, and Doc, and Ricardo, and all the others, and—Gracia. He didn't want to think of Gracia.

Pablo lifted a face gray and grinning, with blood cascading down it from a new wound on his face. "By the saints, *Jefe*," he called, "let us do that. And I think I have seen Bautista, called El Diablo there. If we kill him, our welcome in Paradise is most sure!" He crossed himself swiftly.

But Lars' thick, raging voice cried out. "What is matter? Ve talk like cackling hens! Yumpin' rattlesnakes! For vy do we wait?"

Silver saw that a circle of dark red was spreading over his shoulder and chest, and from the peak of his yellow hair a scarlet stream ran downward to stain his eyebrows and drip below.

Silver lifted on an elbow and opened his mouth to say, "Let's go!" But the sharply wicked crack of a Winchester cut him off.

Silver turned, to see a figure silhouetted against the late light swing down from a horse a hundred yards away and rush forward from cover to cover.

"Damn!" he said softly.

The figure lanced downslope, darting, while the fire from below still snarled.

"Get them," Silver snapped. "Keep down that shootin' an' give him a chance."

HE LIFTED sideways of his rock, thumbing newly loaded guns in a continuous staccato roar. His ears told him that Lars and Pablo also had settled to this work.

Behind them, the Winchester whipped out its venom at intervals, coming closer, and then all at once a panting form flung itself down by Silver's side. It was Bill Lang.

"What in hell you doin' here?"

"I—I couldn't take it." Bill Lang's eyes met the coolness in Silver's gaze with glacier ice of their own. "Too many against you. An' I didn't like that business at the state line."

Silver stared at him. "Look, Ranger—you've put yourself in a jackpot. Can't you see we're holdin' deuces here."

Bill Lang's grin was tight. "It's a rigged deck, *hombre*," he said. "You think I'm scareder to die than you are?"

Silver warmed suddenly. "I never thought I'd get this out of a lawman. You're in for hell from the Rangers if you ever get out of this."

Bill Lang laughed without mirth. "Look," he said, showing his ripped shirt. "I made Zeke a present of my badge before I crossed the line."

Silver fought a sudden tightness in his throat. Then his face hardened. "You come in time, son," he said grimly. "We're just moving forward."

He saw Bill Lang's breath catch and marked the sudden gleam in his eye. "I didn't make any mistake," the ex-Ranger murmured. "Let's go."

Silver slammed the last fresh cartridge into his burning guns and ripped upward, racing for the next cover forward, with the Colts hammering death at lifted heads.

To the side, Pablo followed, his gray mouth howling sudden blasphemies. A swift, wry grin twisted Silver's mouth at that familiar sound. How many times had he listened to it while lead howled in the air past him? Pablo the Pious—who would knife a man for one word that seemed to him sacrilegious in ordinary times, but who bawled blasphemies that must have made his saints blench every time there was a thorough fight going on.

Ahead of them, a high, hating voice squawled in Spanish, "They're coming forward. Get them. Kill them."

El Diablo was there!—sure of his kill!

"Stand up Bautista!" Silver yelled. "Take first shot, you yellow son! I'll give you that chance."

He lifted from his rock and ran forward, holding his fire. Lead hit him, stunning the nerves of his side.

Behind him, Lars Johanssen yelled, "To hall with this! I'm going to get me some devil meat!"

Lars, who didn't essentially believe that bullets could hurt him! Silver had been afraid of this, in the back of his mind. When the fight got close enough Lars lost his head, went berserk, set out to collect what beef he could with the weight of his hamlike hands.

And then, like a thin, urgent message, a rifle shot sounded far off.

It came from behind and the sawtooth rock-thrust beyond. And it put a stopper on that hell-howl of gunfire as though somebody had corked a popping bottle.

There was a silence that may have endured for one whole heartbeat but which seemed endless, and then the lifting, mocking, deadly cry came from the age-sharpened rocks: "*Al Seelver, los Halcónes*! Hell's Hawks for Trent!"

Magpie! Magpie Myers—ageless, wrinkled and wiser than Satan. Old Magpie, and the brassy, hell-howling voices that lifted in this yell that had ended a thousand savage fights, that had made the name of Silver Trent known, and feared, and loved wherever men spoke Mexican!

He didn't have to ask what they were doing here. They were here because Magpie once again had disregarded orders, once again had watched El Diablo with the relentless eye of a catamount watching a hydrophobia dog. Because Silver Trent's men never doubted that he would save them and never believed that he could manage to save himself!

"A nos otros, los halcónes!" The great rallying yell burst from Silver's exultant throat, and he leaped forward, guns hammering. EL DIABLO'S men broke then, panic-stricken. Broke, to be cut down under that merciless fire from front and rear.

A sudden gust of rage and triumph clutched at Silver's throat.

But he was cheated again. A black-clad twisted figure flashed between two rocks and then was gone. A moment later the pound of racing hoofs sounded. Don Esteben Varro y Bautista had escaped!

Silver stood panting, snarling, as the firing checked, died away. The taste of triumph was suddenly ashes in his mouth.

Beside him a voice drawled quietly, "Looks like I didn't make a bad swap."

Silver looked into Bill Lang's cool amused eyes. He put a hard hand on the ex-Ranger's shoulder. "I'm glad you feel it," he said heavily. "I—I got to get back to Jim Clane."

"I had a look at him," Bill Lang said. "I learned somethin' about doctorin' before I joined up with the Rangers. I figured that he might pull through."

Jim Clane's eyes were open when they got back to him, though his breathing was heavy and gasping. Silver reached a hand toward him.

"How are you, Jim?"

Jim's grin was faint but perceptible. "Better'n I deserve,"

he breathed. "Hell, you—don't think a little—lead like this—would—"

Silver said swiftly. "He still needs a doctor. Where's—"

Bill Lang snapped. "Never mind, he'll get well with one," he said. "Hell, *hombre.* Maybe a Ranger can't cross the Border, but if a medico cain't, my gun will want to know why."

The reckless, welcoming yells of Silver's men were in his ears, so that his heart beat a little faster, but his eyes were steady on Bill Lang. "The Rangers took a job an'—an' a bum dream—away from me," Silver murmured, "but they shore as hell made up for it—an' a little bit more, too!"

Bill Lang grinned at him suddenly as he turned away. "I'll be back," he said, "with the best damn doctor either side of El Paso!"

A reeling hook-nosed gun-freighted figure appeared from the ruck of Silver's men. "An' here he is!" boomed the great whiskey-hoarse voice of Doc Brimstone. "Rest yourself, while I get at this redheaded rapscallion."

Silver grinned at Bill Lang. "He's right, Bill. The best either side of the Border—drunk or sober."

Bill Lang's grin was full of sudden baffled admiration. "I might have knowed… Somethin' tells me I'm not goin' to miss the Rangers a-tall."

Silver's faint smile answered him. "Me either," he said softly.

GUN-DOCTOR
FOR THE DAMNED

EXCEPTING FOR the drunk at the corner table, the cantina was empty of customers. The proprietor, Pedro Morales, hummed softly to himself behind the bar as he polished glasses. Pedro felt good that morning, even better than usual, and that was very good, for he was a plump, contented man with the shine of good living on his face and a good round belly to help in the proof of it.

And why shouldn't he feel happy? Did he not regularly go to confession at the little adobe mission as a Christian should, and had he not a prospering bar and a good wife who was neither lazy nor barren? No more barren than the gentle goats who multiplied and grew into a proper herd out on the hills in the care of his eldest son.

Maybe one day he might retire from the cantina spending his old age in the sun and the peace of the hills, free forever of the ruction and violence of this bar.

As he thought that, he cast a troubled glance at the *borrachón* in the corner. This drunk seemed harmless enough, but sometimes a sudden mad savagery overtook such a one and made him dangerous. And this *hombre* was big, even though he walked with one shoulder down-hung which made him look smaller.

Pedro would have felt better could he have had a clear look

Lead snarled past Trent's ears, chugging into the adobe behind him....

at his face, but the head waggled always downward under the shadow of the big sombrero.

A peon of the hills, Pedro judged. Certainly not of those who exacted weekly tribute from poor men such as he. Not, that was to say of El Diablo's men. Too well Pedro knew their swaggering sort. Their drunkenness was bold and brutal, but never sodden like this, else their humped master from Hell would have seen them slayed alive....

The door to the cantina kitchen burst open and Maria waddled in, her face blazing with excitement. "Pedro—husband!"

she cried. "We have saved it. The sale of my young *pollios* has brought the last silver we needed."

Her joyful eyes swept the room and seeing only the drunk in the corner she held out her cupped hands which were full of silver and a few gold pieces. *"Mira!"* she cried. "Look! It is enough for the shrine!"

Behind her, a boy of ten or eleven had entered and stood at the end of the bar, black eyes blazing at his father out of a face which quivered with emotion. Following him came a ragtag of younger ones, including a toddler who pulled at the mother's skirts, caught uncomprehendingly by her excitement.

She turned on them fiercely, *"Vaya!"* she cried. "Back to the kitchen, all of you. You know you are not allowed in the cantina!"

They gave back, even the toddler, looking at her out of wondering eyes, not believing this order, and then surged again toward her as she turned her back. Only the boy at the end of the bar turned to obey.

"No, not thou, Pedrocito," she said, "since thou art old enough to understand." And then she turned on her husband, whose plump face was shining with the same excitement which transformed her own. "See, we can have it now—the shrine to our sacred mother, Mary, who has blessed us so richly. At last the money is here—to the last peso—saved. Oh, Pedro!"

Pedro took the money from her hand, putting it on the bar, and swept her into his arms.

"Gracias a Dios!" he exclaimed. "Thanks to God!"

"Gracias a Santa Maria, tambien," she reproved him gently.

And then her enthusiasm took her again, so that she pushed him a little away and cried, "Think! Think how it will look, there in our bedroom, the beautiful, golden shrine! No one in all Villa Maria will be able to worship so well!"

"That is pride, my little one," he rebuked her. The drunk got up from his chair and weaved over toward the bar.

It was young Pedrocito who said fiercely, *"Que quiere, hombre?"* suspicious because the stranger was getting too close to the money.

The drunk disregarded the question, peering at the silver on the bar.

Pedro swept it out of sight, glaring, and then snatched at the ancient single-barreled shotgun behind the bar.

THE BOY, Pedrocito, flung himself suddenly at the stranger, kicking and clawing furiously. *"Borrachón!"* he yelled. "Drunken son of a pig! Gutter scum! Your cursed father and mother were—"

He broke off as his mother's gentle hand pulled him back. "Quiet, niño," she said firmly.

"But no," her husband protested. "Leave the boy alone. He is right." He turned angrily on the stranger. "You! Get out of my cantina!"

Maria was staring wide-eyed at the back of the drunk who was stumbling back to his table. For, as he turned, the man had shot her one warm-gray glance from under his sombrero. She was to remember that strangely enigmatic look later.... But at the moment, the opening of the batwing doors took her attention.

The three men who swaggered in were decorated with double cartridge belts about their waists, from which hung holstered Colts. About their torsos were draped other cartridge belts out of which the flattened leaden ends of Winchester bullets looked grimly.

"And what's this talk about money, friend Pedro?" the leader asked, and the grin on his narrow lips was cruel.

Maria was suddenly desperately frightened, and Pedro's face had gone the color of sun-dried putty.

"I—I—" the proprietor stammered.

"You—you—!" the leader of the three mocked him. And reaching out, he slapped Pedro's face.

"We heard you were making a little too much money," he snarled. "Been holding out on us, eh? We'll soon stop that. Give me that money, witless one, and pray to your God that our master will not punish you too greatly."

Hands shaking, Pedro gathered up the coins and handed it over the bar. Maria screaming like a woman in pain, snatched at his hands.

"No, señors," she cried frenziedly at the three. "You do not understand. This is the money of the blessed—"

The open palm of the twisted-faced man put a loud period to her speech, as Pedrocito uttered an anguished animal-like cry and surged forward.

"Cabeza! Look out!" It was the third of the trio who yelled that and whirled, stabbing for his guns.

He whirled toward the drunk at the table, who was not any longer a drunk, who had whipped to his feet, letting his concealing *serape* drop from shoulders. His hands had blurred toward shoulder holsters and had come out loaded with sudden lightning.

The third man's cry and the lifting flick of his gun did none of that three a service.

"Hold it," the ex-drunk said crisply. But that was too late, for the third man's fast draw was coming up.

The *borrachón* shot once, and the bullet thudded audibly into flesh.

The second of the trio, less absorbed than the twisted Cabeza, was next in that hell-filled moment. His draw was oiled and deadly as the strike of a snake, but Pedrocito hit him, his charge not stopped.

The *borrachón*—this man who had seemed only a drunken peon from the hills—felt the slug snarl past his ears. In the same instant he saw the twisted face of Cabeza become a bloody tangle of flesh from his own bullet.

Maria's sobbing breath was a moan of sorrow and relief. But the boy was staring wide-eyed at the big man whose guns still smoked in his hands.

The ex-drunk, whose powerful shoulders had lost their crippled twist, was looking now at the three bodies on the floor. His gray eyes were troubled as his swift fingers shoved fresh cartridges into his guns. Holstering his weapons then, he shoved his sombrero back from his forehead. The movement revealed a single thick white lock of hair running diagonally away from his forehead.

Pedrocito's breath went in in a gasp and out in a triumphant cry: *"Seelver! Es Seelver Trent! El Halcón! El Halcón de las Sierras!"*

The big man turned suddenly quiet gray eyes on him. "Yes,

son," he said quietly in Spanish. "The Hawk—as you say. Be not afraid."

But Pedrocito scarcely heard him. His eyes were lost in awe. *"El Halcón!"* he breathed. "And I—" he touched himself unbelievingly on the chest— *"Madre de Dios!* I called him a drunken pig!"

From outside horses' hoofs pounded. Voices snarled, *"Que pasa?* What has happened?"

Silver's words were swift, warning Pedro and Maria, "Get down! Keep out of this!" And he whirled toward the door.

AS HE ran, he cursed himself. He had not meant to start anything here. This was to have been merely a trip of exploration. It was not the attempted theft of the money that had set him off and wrecked his carefully laid plans. It was that slap on Maria's face.

Silver Trent had meant to collect the money afterwards. Along with all the rest of the tribute that Bautista, who was called El Diablo, collected from this town.

The plan had been made because of Pablo, the Pious, who prayed in peace and cursed in war and, after Magpie Myers, was Trent's right hand man.

Pablo had said, with a kind of quiet insistence, "This El Diablo, he is not content with his riches. He collects tribute from all the towns. Every little merchant, every cantina owner or *zapato*-maker, must pay a fixed percentage of his earnings. This is so in the pueblo of Villa Maria, every week, on Saturday. If we went there, we could collect from the collectors, and return the money to the townspeople. Maybe then El Diablo would tire of his game. Or try to make a trap for us, into which he, himself, might fall."

Trent could remember Magpie Myers glaring at him. "This town ain't nothin' but a terbaccer-spit on the face of the earth," he announced drily. "Why go there?"

"Because," Pablo had said firmly, "it is the town of my aunt."

Silver had gulped his laughter into a throat which hid behind an impassive face. These curious surprises were typical of Pablo, about whom even he, Trent, knew little. But there had been something somehow unbelievable and comic in the fact that Pablo, the long-faced, the religious ascetic, the wild fighting man, should have so mundane and human a thing as an aunt But it was so, and so he had accepted.

Only, the plan had been laid to collect the money from the collectors outside of town.

In that way, there would he no blame for the townsfolk. In that way they might suffer nothing from El Diablo's blood-thirsty wrath.

And in accordance with that plan. Silver had left his men outside the town. He himself had gone in disguised as a drunken hill-peon in order to check up on the collections. Later he was to rejoin his band and take Diablo's men on the out-trail.

But the plan had misfired. Maria, desperate over the loss of her shrine, and slapped in the bargain, had had no place in the original idea.

Well, the *habas* were spilled now, and badly spilled, to judge by the number of voices outside. For just an instant Trent entertained the notion of going out the back way, but that would be to leave Pedro and Maria to face the music, to explain why Bautista's coyotes had been killed. Better for them if he went out front, because that would give El Diablo a victim, somebody to chase, and nobody to put to the question.

ALL THIS ran through his mind before and while he raced toward the bat-wing doors of the cantina, knowing well that he was going to run into bullets as he charged out.

Even after their voices, the number of them surprised him as he plunged into the brilliant daylight and dodged sideways crouching. Diablo might send collectors, but not this many. He had run into a trap!

The street was filled with mounted gunmen, and lead snarled past Trent's ears, chugging into the adobe behind him.

He broke back, his guns hammering against his palms as he zigzagged.

As always his fire was deadly accurate and it is probable that fact which saved his life. The Bautista gunmen, dismounting, were grouped awkwardly, and the slug that cut into them had a shrewd way of cutting; down the guns that were most dangerous to the life of Silver Trent.

But the odds were desperate, and this was not a street but a plaza. Backing, Silver remembered that the alleyway behind him led only back into the square. To back into that would be to put himself into a trap in which he would be attacked from in front and behind.

A hammering snarl of gunfire sounded behind him and voices raised in a shout *"En avanti, los halcónes! Hell's Hawks for Trent!"*

His own men! It struck instant confusion into the ranks of

El Diablo's warriors. They had been up against the Trent crowd before and had no great stomach for it.

A swift glance over his shoulder showed Silver that all of them—at least all he had brought with him—were on the charge. Magpie and Jim Clane and Lars and Ricardo and Bill Lang and Pablo himself were racing into the square, guns blazing.

The Bautista men gave back. One of them yelled something that Silver could not catch and, after a moment of confusion, it seemed to him that several of them had disappeared.

He did not follow them. The odds were too great for a standout gunfight. He would lose too many of his men. He worked toward a clump of ornamental bushes and a statue which offered some cover at the edge of the square. Twenty to six was too many.

His men, seeing him zigzag across to cover, swerved and ran toward him. But by now the Bautista renegades realized how few they were. They pressed forward, following what they thought to be a retreat.

A snarl of gunfire spat from the alleyway on his flank. The Bautista men had seen their advantage and had done the one thing they could to make the victory sure. This enfilade fire was deadly.

CHAPTER 2
WHEN DEATH STOPS BY

S ILVER HEARD Lars Johanssen's involuntary grunt as lead struck him. And then a crease of fire like a whip across his shoulders told him of a bullet which had narrowly missed his own life.

For one brief moment, hesitation held him. And in that moment, a figure burst out of Pedro Morales' cantina. The scrawny, blazing-eyed figure of a boy of ten or eleven, with an ancient single-barreled shotgun in his hands.

Pedrocito had also seen that flank attack, had understood what it meant to his hero, Silver Trent. Pedrocito, who had sinned in his own eyes by having attacked and cursed the great man who was the idol of every poor man's son on both sides of the Border—Pedrocito had seized his father's old fowling piece and charged to the rescue.

The rusted weapon went off, the kick of it nearly knocking the slender form over. A howl of pain sounded from the alleyway as the birdshot found their mark. There was silence for half a heartbeat, and then came the vicious blasting hammer of Colt-fire.

The boy's body whipped like a willow branch in a hard gust of wind. The muzzle of the shotgun swept upward then down, as the piece fell from his hands. He crumpled pitifully at the knees and his light body made a small heartbreaking smack on cobblestones which reddened instantly.

A curse tore out of Silver's tightened throat. "Damn them!" he half sobbed, "Damn them for not men, but the groveling spawn of Hell itself!" Then his powerful body whipped upward, crouching. "Get them!" he yelled "By God, get them, if there's a drop of blood in your veins!"

Lars' furious bellow met his own and Jim Clane's snarling curse and the spine-chilling furious rebel yell which was Magpie's warcry.

Silver and Lars jumped toward the alleyway. The others drove forward.

No need here to advance and take cover while the rifle fire of the other squads behind covered them. They slammed forward under the cruel, deadly cover of their own sixgun fire. Six men against a score.

One of the men who had shot the boy lanced to his feet, eyes suddenly desperate, head turning to show him the way to run. Silver's lead cut him down. Another half-rose, gun leveled, eyes glaring death over the sights. The slug from Silver's left-hand gun hit squarely between the eyes, so that the thing they buried would have no bridge to its nose.

A third of that group fell to Lars Johanssen's guns and another man spun, hit in the shoulder. That was in the first dodging run, when they fought as expert gun-fighters should fight. But with Lars, that could not last. This blond giant believed himself impervious to gunfire, against all the evidence, and when the enemy got close he always went berserk, forgetting to shoot, and going in with his bare hands.

He did that now. He slammed both guns savagely at the faces of the two remaining men. One missed; the other hit a gunman in the chest, knocking him backwards. The first gunman leveled his six-shooter at Lars but the hammer clicked on a fired chamber. With a squawk of terror he turned to run.

Silver swerved then, racing toward the support of his other men, but Lars kept on in great leaping strides.

There was a coldness in Silver's spine, despite his long experience in battle. Because he knew Lars loved children and had a heart choked with hot and hating rage in this moment he was not altogether sane, and he knew Lars would overtake that fleeing gunman. And in Silver's ears, even before it happened, was the low, flash-muffled crack of that man's neck.

SILVER, HOWEVER, flashing forward with his hot guns hammering, did not care as much as he might have. Whoever worked for El Diablo was by definition a heartless, ruthless and cruel brute, worthy of any shameful death. And the renegades, giving back, pale-faced, before the savage assault were his business now.

The sixth cartridge in his right-hand gun slammed into a Bautista man, spinning him. And then they broke, Silver's blazing-eyed figure being just enough to turn the balance.

They ran, helter-skelter, diving into doorways, into the spaces between windows, jumping for roofs, until, all at once, the street and the plaza were clear.

Silver ran for the boy. Maria was beside him now and Pedro, emerging pale-faced from the cantina, was coming toward him.

Gently, Silver thrust the sobbing mother aside. The boy had been hit in the body twice, once in the leg. He was bleeding badly, and his eyes were glazed as dying men's are glazed.

Expertly Silver's fingers probed the wounds, his eyes estimating the angle at which the bullets had entered and the probable damage.

"Go get the local medico and get him fast," he snapped at Pedro. Then, infinitely careful, he lifted Pedrocito in his arms and carried him into the cantina.

This was bad, he knew. If the kid lived it would be almost a miracle. Yet he had to stop and see, and had to hold his men here, although that was a risk that none of them should take.

El Diablo's men did not quit easily. They would be back, and there would be more of them. On second thought, he had no right to hold his saddle-mates here.

He faced them as they crowded in, seeing the blood that stained several shirts and watching how they supported Ricardo among them.

"Look, *amigos,*" he said crisply. "Get out and get clear. That gang is going to be back pronto. You can't do anything more here."

They looked at him, staring. But it was Ricardo who spoke first, his lean hawk's face pale, but reckless despite the fact that he could hardly stand.

"And you?" he questioned fiercely. "You come?"

Silver shrugged, his eyes veiled. "In a little while," he promised placatingly. "I'll wait until the doctor comes." Then his head lifted and his eyes were cold, facing them. "Go now!"

It was an order that they would have obeyed unquestiontngly, as they obeyed all his orders, under circumstances. But now Ricardo's faint laugh was almost a sneer. "To hell with that, *Jefe,*" he murmured and slumped, unconscious.

And Magpie said, his breath still coming fast from the fight and his ancient, leathery face a little pale. "Plenty hell with that, Silver! We stick with you to the last damn' shell!"

The others growled, backing him up.

Lars came in, his great hands flexing and his blue eyes a little ashamed. He was again himself—a man who would not crack the neck of a chuckawalla except when the madness of battle was on him. But then his eyes fell on Pedrocito's slender, broken figure and the shame went out of his eyes, the blaze of fury replacing it. And there was a mastiff snarl in the thick column of his throat.

The town doctor came and made his examination. Afterwards, he emitted an excited volley of technical terms. "Señor," he ended abjectly, turning moist palms up to Silver, "I can not do such an operation. There is only one man in all this section of Mexico who can save this boy's life."

SILVER LOOKED at him, the slate gray of his eyes thoughtful and full of regret. "Two," he murmured, thinking then of Doc Brimstone. But Doc Brimstone was three hundred miles away, with the rest of the gang.

Silver had sent them off on a raid of one of El Diablo's mines, coming himself to take care of this small matter of the mulcting of Villa Maria, the town of Pablo's aunt, out of respect for that fighting and pious lieutenant of his. That had been a mistake, as he now saw. Someway, El Diablo must have gotten wind of the thing, and had sent men to trap him.

His cold eyes slapped at the doctor. "And the other?" he demanded.

The medico wrung his hands. "Señor," he cried, "it is the personal physician of El Diablo—I mean to say, of Don Esteban Bautista y Gonzales."

Silver's hands, powerful as steel grappling hooks caught his shoulders, shook him savagely.

"What trick is this, dog and son of a dog?" he snarled.

The Mexican trembled like a reed in the wind, his brown eyes helpless and terrified as a spaniel's in the grip of a mountain lion.

"Señor! I but say the truth, and may God punish me if I lie. He—he is not a good man, this Doctor Snaipo. B-but he is of the best in both medicine and surgery. Don Esteban would have only the best. Señor—señor! I beg you...."

Silver released him slowly. "What you say must be true," he muttered. He turned on his men. "Well?" he asked. "The decision rests with you."

Jim Clane laughed aloud, his quick hands going by instinct to the butts of his guns and his red hair seeming to flame in the gloom of this cantina.

"By God!" he breathed exultantly. "By God, Silver—even if it wasn't for the kid, it couldn't be missed."

And Magpie Myers grinned, his ageless blue eyes twinkling. "I think you got an idee there, son!" he murmured.

But Bill Lang said slowly, "I ain't shore I get it, Silver. Are you meanin to go an' take this sawbones, whatever his name is? Can you get away with that?"

Silver said quietly. "No, Bill. Nobody can. There ain't but six of us, an' this place is guarded like a fort. I wouldn't ask any man to try it, unless...."

Bill Lang's face flushed suddenly, deeply. "Look, *amigo*," he said. "I—I'm kind of new, like you know. In the Rangers we tried some tough things, but we never took anything on without knowin' what it was or whether if could be done. If I spoke out of turn, why put it down to greenness. Anything you an' the rest say is all right by me."

Silver's grin at him was sudden and warm. *"Amigo,"* he said softly, "here we go! To let El Doctor Snaipo make our acquaintance."

Pablo's deep sigh put an exultance across the quiet air. *"Dios!"* he murmured. "I have served a man! And by the Grace of Mary he becomes always more a man! Let us go now—in the name of the blessed saints!"

Silver turned on the medico, his voice crackling, "Keep the kid alive, or I'll have your hide. Take care of Ricardo also, and tell him I said to stay on guard here until we get back."

To Maria, he said gently, "Be of good hope, mother of men. We will come back."

CHAPTER 3
IN THE DEVIL'S PLAYGROUND

THERE WERE others in northern Mexico who had haciendas—great estates, and great houses, but there was only one who had a castle which was also a great stone fortress. Don Esteban Bautista y Gonzales lived in a valley surrounded by mountains. There weren't many ways to get in, and once in, it was not easy to get across the deep-grassed flats to the hacienda, which itself flanked by its gardens, backed against the sheer wall of a ravine.

Even the trail itself was a danger to Silver Trent and his crew. The feud between Trent and Bautista, between the Hawk and the Devil, had ran long enough to be classic along this Borderland. It had been affair of blow and counterblow, of advantage first one way and then another.

Silver Trent had balked El Diablo of the revolution which would have made him undisputed master of most of northern Mexico. He lad checked him in a hundred fights and skirmishes. But, also, he had lost more than once. Fighting as he did, an outlaw, with only a comparatively few men, against a man who was more of an outlaw than he, but who yet contrived to stay— by bribery and sheer force of his riches—within the technical protection of the Mexican law—fighting thus, Trent was always at an enormous disadvantage.

Yet because his own two score men were recruited from the best of the hard-case *hombres* from either side of the Border, Trent had managed somehow to win most of the tricks in this deadly-game.

But the time had come now when Silver Trent's cold patience was wearing thin. Deep inside him he had the growing weakness of irritation because he had not yet succeeded in killing Bautista. A stubborn sense of fair play had forced him to give even chances to the man who never thought of giving him an even chance in return. It was a danger he felt in himself—a danger which might any day cause him to overplay his hand, because of the hatred that grew in him and the conviction that obsessed him that this land could never be clean until El Diablo was sent back to the Hell from which he had emerged.

The quietness of his men, following him along this trail, was proof enough that they felt in him a mood that endangered both him and themselves. A kid had been hurt, to begin with. And that alone was something that Trent could not stand.

Coupled with his obsessive hatred of El Diablo, it put a frozen recklessness in him, a furious, reckless rage which might at any moment plunge them all into disaster.

They had ridden with him gladly, because they were murderously angry themselves, and because their lives were made up of danger and daring beyond the ordinary. But as their blood cooled and their good fighting sense took possession of them, they began to cast uneasy glances at Trent and to exchange warning glances among themselves.

Silver himself, riding in front, was oblivious to all this. He was fighting the helpless, murderous rage in him.

He was half unconscious of the trail and what was before them, yet he instinctively set the pace expertly, to get the best out of the least able and enduring of their horses.

It was by instinct, too, that he set his own powerful bay scrambling up a high place in the trail, and from that point saw Bautista's men coming back. Had his instinct and subconscious calculation been wrong, they would have been betrayed into disaster, but because his movement was right, they were enabled to draw off the trail and watch some half a hundred men go by.

When they had passed, Bill Lang drew a long breath and murmured, "Maybe I haven't been havin' enough confidence.

SILVER STARED at him blankly and led the way up the trail. He wondered what Bill Lang meant. Did Lang think that this was all of El Diablo's force? If so, he was a lot mistaken.

A turn in the tortuous trail showed a momentary glimpse of a narrow slot in a wall of granite—the entrance to the valley.

Silver called a halt. It would have been better to detour, to come in another way, but there was no time. That kid might die for a matter of minutes.

He looked over his crew. It was a pity Ricardo was not here, for he could move like a Yaqui shadow. So, for that matter, could Magpie. But Magpie was old, and this meant hard climbing, and fast, exhausting work. For that type of work the others would be useless. He looked at Magpie speculatively.

The oldster glared back at him. "I'm a better man than you are, and will be when I'm a hundred," he growled.

Silver grinned and swung down from his horse.

Before they got above the guards in the pass, Magpie was breathing loud enough to call out all the reserves on the Bautista hacienda, but he had made no other sound, and he smiled sardonically at the rock that rolled suddenly under Silver's boots.

He said nothing, but the swift nod of his white head said, "Better move fast." And Silver swung himself down over the ledge.

He hit the shoulders of a guard who had just begun to look up, and the man hurtled downward. His face hit the rocks with the sound of a thrown tomato and he lay still. The other guard grabbed for his Winchester which stood against the rock wall, and Magpie's hard-breathing voice stopped him like a death-rattle. "Don't try it, *hombre!*"

The man froze, looking upward, and Silver went to him.

A moment later the hills heard a sound seldom heard this soon before the set of sun—the wild half-human scream of a mountain lion, thrice repeated. And ten seconds afterwards, the other three appeared, riding after him down the trail.

Afterwards, there was a devious, silent trail through arroyos across the flat-lands along which Silver led them. Behind him, Lars Johanssen grinned broadly, remembering a time when he and Silver had been imprisoned here, with Jim and the girl, Gracia, and of the things that followed.

Looking at the house from where the arroyo gave cover near to the north garden, Silver frowned. The place was too quiet. There should have been more men around, more easy, casual movement. Were the rest of Diablo's men gone somewhere?

His blood began to pound suddenly in his veins. Bautista had suspected something in Villa Maria today, had had more men there than he should have had. Could there be some leak in Silver's own crowd? If that was so, might it not be that El Diablo had learned of the raid which the rest of Silver's men were conducting. He might even now have arranged a trap.

Grim-faced, he decided that there was only one thing to do—win or lose—to jump this gray faced fortress at the gallop. Storm it now—and quickly!

He turned to his men. "We'll go out now," he said grimly. "Two to the front, two to the side door. Bill Lang will stay with the horses. Jim Clane will go with me to the front. Lars and Magpie to the side. Move fast and don't let anything stop you!"

He put the bay to the steep slope of the arroyo and slammed toward the house.

A startled Mexican yelled sharply as he pulled up at the door and swung down from the saddle. The man had a gun at his side so Silver whipped toward him and slammed his tight fist into his jaw.

INSIDE, THE gloom of the house buzzed with sudden life. A wild-eyed man burst out of a side door and Silver cut him down with a slap of a Colt barrel behind his ear. Another, farther down the great hall squawked and hurtled toward the door which Silver knew led to Diablo's enormous living room. The men who dived in carommed off another who was coming out, staggered and disappeared. But the fellow he had bumped stood there, half-breathless, wholly uncomprehending.

Silver seized him in grip which bit into the man's biceps so that he winced.

Outside, at the side of the house, gunfire burst in a spiteful snarl, then ceased.

"Where's the doctor?" Silver snapped at the man he held in his grip. "Talk, *hombre,* and talk fast and true, because the buzzards are looking for you."

The man goggled at him, wild-eyed. "But señor," he stammered, "The doctor is upstairs. I—"

"Where upstairs?"

"At the left of the stairs. The—the last room, señor, I—*ugh!*"

That final grunt was because Silver had lifted him by the

scruff of the neck and the seat of the pants and hurled him toward the stairs. "Show us," he snarled, "and God help you if you've lied!"

Whimpering, the man ran before him, turned left at the top of the stairs and started to point. The door opened.

A great, emaciated giant of a man with an enormous head looked at him. He must have been many inches over six feet, for he towered over Silver, and his dome-like forehead topped the face of a petulant and shrewd child.

"You're El Doctor Snaipo?" Silver snarled at him.

The giant looked dazed and at the same time filled with a curious pride. "You know me?" he asked.

Silver took him by an arm and slammed him against the corridor wall, so that if he had not been wholly stunned by surprise before, he was now, owing to the contact of his head against that solid plaster.

"Get all his tools," he snapped to Jim Clane. "Come on, you!" This last to Snaipo.

It was as simple as that. Racing out the front door, with the medico held between them, and the two who had come in the side way with them, they had only one man to kill—one of Bautista's gunmen—a beak-nosed snarling devil who had more perverse loyalty than wisdom.

That, and the arroyo, and then El Diablo's squawling yell behind them, as belatedly he found out what had happened and summoned those men he had kept with him.

Silver turned and saw the hunched, spiderly, black-clad figure cursing there in the afternoon light. His jaw set and his pulses hammered with a violence that visibly shook him.

El Diablo was too far away for accurate Colt fire. But he was there and not well enough guarded. A quick charge now, a fast deadly fight, and Silver might get him. But there was the kid to think of.

They had gotten Snaipo, and very likely they could get away now. A dozen men were boiling out of the bunkhouse at the far side of the hacienda. To risk a fight would be to endanger a child's life—a kid who had a fighting heart as big as his great brown eyes.

Yet there was time for a rifle shot. One cold and flawless shot would put a leaden slug through this devil's head....

SILVER STOOD with his nails biting into his palms, shaking with the intensity of this desire. But the curious stubborn reluctance he had held him back. He had to kill this man in a fair fight. It was absurd, he realized. It was ironical. It was infinitely stupid, almost criminal. But it was so.

Bill Lang however, had no such romantic ideas. As a Ranger, a criminal was to him a criminal, a snake something to be stomped on when necessary. And he knew the use of a rifle.

In the quivering second during which Silver hesitated, Bill's hand whipped to the Winchester in his saddle boot. He slapped the butt to his shoulder, his eye flashing along the sights.

Magpie's hand slapped the barrel up.

"You got plenty to learn," he growled deep in his throat.

El Diablo was Silver's meat or no man's. Not to mention the

fact that when Silver did not shoot or command the others to, there was no shooting.

"But—" the ex-Ranger protested.

At Magpie's side, Pablo said acidly. "You have a head, perhaps. Gringo. Try to use it, but do not try to substitute it for *El Jefe's* head."

Bill Lang flushed angrily, but he lowered the rifle.

Silver, oblivious of them, drew a long sigh. "Let's go," he said regretfully, almost as if to himself.

They had brought Ricardo's horse for the doctor and already he had been hoisted into the saddle. They followed the arroyo at a dead run.

Behind them, shouts and the faint pound of hoofs told them that the pursuit was in full cry. Could their already tired horses keep ahead of fresh ones? And if they did, there were half a hundred men in the two ahead of them. They were caught between two forces, and outnumbered twelve to one. What chance had they?

"One damn shot might have made this difference," Bill Lang snarled aloud.

Riding beside him, Pablo said coldly, "Fool! I begin to tire of you. You talk overmuch."

The ex-Ranger's hand flashed toward his gun in a movement that blurred like the spokes of a racing buggy wheel as he cursed Pablo.

Pablo's hand also moved, but the thing was too fast to show as a blur.

"Finish your draw, *amigo*," he said softly, the razor blade of his knife jiggling at Bill Lang's throat as their racing mounts pounded off-stride.

Bill's hand froze with the Colt half out of leather. His hard eyes glared, un-scared, at Pablo.

"It's easier and faster to pull a knife, *hombre,*" he said bitterly. "Maybe we'll try again sometime when you're a little farther off."

Pablo whipped the blade back into its sheath, and turned his head toward the arroyo road again. "When you wish, and when the blessed saints consent," he said tranquilly.

CHAPTER 4
FIGHT AND DIE!

THE TOWN of Villa Maria lay silent in the sunset under a pall of fear. On an ordinary day the streets and cantinas would have been crowded by those who had finished the day's work, and would be now about the real pursuit of the Mexican soul—pleasure. The joys of leisure, lazy and nonchalant, of drink and gay talk, and of food and gambling—of, in fact, all the charming and delightful preliminaries to that time when kisses would be ardent through the warm and gentle dark.

Just now, grim-faced men, their mouths and eyes cruel above the array of weapons which decorated them, had taken possession of the town. They had raided first the cantina of Pedro Morales, and finding it empty had begun angrily to search the town. As a result of that search more than one peaceable citizen nursed an ear sore from deafening slap or a nose broken by the vicious cut of a gunbarrel. And one man, insane in the wish to protect his wife, was dead.

The Villa Marians kept to their houses and kept silent. This town knew well the men of El Diablo. It had paid tribute for a year and a day of weeks.

"We are humble men, *amigos*," they said. "If it is not the government, it is someone like this Don Esteban and his bravos. Of what use to complain? The wise man keeps silent and thanks the good God for a tortilla and a mouthful of wine. That your children may grow to greatness, compadre, and you yourself to the contentment of a hundred years! *Salud!*"

But these swaggering renegades who ranged this town, demanding free wine and tequila from the cantinas, bullying its citizens, laying brutal hands on any señorita unwise enough to show herself, were not content. It appeared that those they sought were well-hidden. The men of Silver Trent had certainly left—no doubt they had even taken with the Pedro Morales, his wife and children and the wounded man who had certainly been too badly hit to travel unassisted.

Also, it appeared, they had taken the corpse of the boy who had had the criminal audacity to assist outlaws in their wickedness, and who had been well riddled with lead for his pains. Let that be a lesson to the townspeople....

Meanwhile, Silver, halting his men in the willows by the Rio Amarillo, sniffed the air like a wolf scenting danger from afar. His eyes showed hard and thoughtful. Once, he cast a considering look over his shoulder at the backtrail, where El Diablo and his men, distanced by trail-guile and excellent horse-flesh, must still be close.

Pablo's hand fell on his arm. "Look, *Jefe*," his murmur came. "There is a little one who plays behind the far house. Let me go. In this way, I will find out all that can be known."

Silver nodded and Pablo shucked off cartridge belts and guns and boots and silver embroidered jacket.

In five minutes he was back, and the quintette, leading the tall medico between them, began to move. Outwardly careless, inwardly tense, weapons concealed, they moved by back ways to the house where Pedrocito and Ricardo and Pedro and Maria and the town medico were concealed.

They were greeted by a gray-faced townsman and his wife, who admitted them in obvious terror, and then opened a trap door into a stinking hole below the house where Pedrocito and the others had been hiding from the search.

AT SILVER'S quick order, they brought the boy up. And then Silver turned to Dr. Snaipo, gun in hand. "Doctor," he said quietly, "I hear that you are good. You had better be. Because if this boy dies, you die. That's the situation which Fate and your own damn rottenness has put you into. So I think that you had better go to work quickly and be better than you have ever been." The words had a quiet deadliness in them and nobody but a born fool would have thought they were not meant.

But this gaunt, high man with his childish, petulant face merely looked at him resentfully. "I do not give treatment under compulsion," he said, and his manner, which might have been bombastic in another man, was impressive in him because of the childish simplicity in it. He added, as a child might speak to a younger child, "I am a great physician."

Silver Trent stared at him, and for once in a long career of knowing exactly what to do, his men saw his eyes baffled. For this man understood the threat of his gun and no doubt knew that it was real, but that reality had no effect on him. He was concerned with other things. Bullets would surely reach him, kill him, but the threat of them would have no effect on the peculiar mentality which lived behind that immature face.

The realization of it stunned Silver. He had kidnapped this man at the risk not only of his own life but that of his men. He had brought him into a town which was a death-trap for any Trent rider. He had gotten him into this house, apparently unseen, by a sort of miracle. He had succeeded in the impossible.... And yet he was beaten.

His quick, sure instinct knew it. And his men, too, sensed it. The silence in that bare, adobe-floored room was as taut as the soundless stretch of a hangman's rope.

Silver drew a sudden, shuddering breath and his finger tightened suddenly on the trigger of his gun. Never in his life before had he committed cold-blooded murder. But he was ready to do it now. If this elongated travesty of a man wished to let a little boy die, then he also would die.

But Dr. Snaipo was unaware both of Silver's glance and the whitening of his trigger finger. Nothing told him that death brushed him with invisible wings. His sulky eyes, enormous and green in his great domed head—his eyes had turned indifferently to the silent, pale-faced figure of Pedrocito breathing faintly, spasmodically there at his side.

They brushed him, those indifferent, unmoral, uncaring eyes, from head to foot, without interest. And then, as Silver's reluctance to do murder fought with his straining trigger finger, El Doctor Snaipo's gaze sharpened.

He bent forward suddenly. "Why," he said suddenly, "it looks as though the bullet had—

He broke off, long jointed, clumsy looking fingers fumbling at the boy's body.

The local medico burst into excited talk "*Sí! Sí!* Doctor!" he cried. "It is so. I told them. Observe that the—"

Dr. Snaipo's impatient gesture cut him off. "Quiet!" he commanded. "Is it for such as you to tell me…?" He turned on Silver and said in a tone which he might have used to a nurse, "Chloroform—either, or some anesthetic. This little one can not stand much shock. And my bag—you brought it, didn't you? Give it to me quickly."

Silver stared at him, stunned.

"Damn you!" El Diablo's medico cried fretfully, his voice in Spanish carrying a curious, heavy accent which Silver had not been able to place. "Will you stand there like an imbecile? Do as I say!"

Silver's gray eyes blazed with sudden humor. "*Sí*, Doctor," he got out in a half-choked voice. He whirled on Jim Clane. "The doc's tools, *hombre!*" he ordered. And then his hand reached for the local medico. "You got chloroform?" he demanded threateningly.

But the town doctor was already moving. "Chloroform! Si, Doctor," he was crying not to Silver but to Snaipo, "I have it!"

A fist pounded on the door and a voice cried, "Open up, in the name of El Presidente!"

THERE WAS an instant silence in the room, then Silver nodded, his smile sardonic. The nod was to his men, who moved with him toward the door. He ripped it open without answering, and the Diablo man outside practically fell in.

Silver, standing aside from the door, reached out and jerked him in. As he did so, a storm of Colt-fire blazed from the buildings behind. Lead snarled through the open doorway, thudding into the wall behind and then splintered the door as Silver slammed it shut.

Silver turned to say something to the man he had pulled in, but the words died on his lips. The man was dead, killed by his comrades' reckless fire.

By that Silver knew that El Diablo himself was in command out there. And he wondered curiously how this man could command any loyalty, even with the money he was prepared to pay to those in his service.

Dr. Snaipo had paid no attention to all this. He was getting his patient ready for the operation.

Silver barred the door and then snapped, "Down—everybody! There's goin' to be plenty gunfire. Keep clear of the door and windows. As for you, Snaipo—"

The doctor did not hear him. And gunfire, smashing in deadly hail through windows and door cut off the rest of his speech.

Snaipo paid no apparent attention to the gunfire. He was busy snarling at his anesthetist, the local medico, who ducked when the hail of lead came through.

A bullet plucked at the tall man's sleeve. He shook his head irritably. "Somebody is shooting in here," he complained. "Tell them not to do that."

Silver glared at him unbelievingly and then he jumped toward the window. "You out there—Bautista!" he bellowed. "We've got your doctor in here. He's operating, and he's in the line of fire. You'll kill him if you keep on shooting, and we'll kill him if he doesn't keep on operating! Call off your dogs until the operation's over."

There was a long moment of silence, then El Diablo's squawling voice lifted. "What are you stopping for?" it caterwauled. "Don't you know we've got the señor that calls himself a Hawk cooped up in there? Hasn't he killed enough of you? Let your guns talk loud, my little ones!"

A storm of gunfire followed his words. Bullets smashed through the splintering door, snarled through the windows pocking the thick adobe walls, and you could hear the thud of those that missed hitting into the outer sides of the house.

Lead snapped at Dr. Snaipo's flanks, cutting his clothing and setting a trail of blood seeping from his lean ribs.

"They are shooting in!" Dr. Snaipo cried querulously. "They should not do that. We must move the patient."

Then, with the others, he moved the table. It was another miracle that none of them took any of the storm of lead that still continued to pour in. And afterwards, Dr. Snaipo was nearly safe. Bullets snarled to one side of him, but only an acutely angled shot could reach him.

Of all this, the man appeared entirely unaware. His long-jointed, clumsy looking hands were moving with the swift, beautiful precision of an accurately made machine.

Silver shook the daze of incredulity out of his mind. All that could be done for Pedrocito had been done. Now his job was to find a way out of the death-trap into which he had recklessly led his men.

THE HALF hour which followed had for him the quality of a bad dream. There was no way out of here. The hideout had been chosen for its hidden cellar hole rather than for its defensive position. The house was open to attack on three sides.

His men knew as much about this situation as he did. And their fire, from the windows and through the crack of the almost useless door, was deadly. Outside, at the angles of the surrounding houses and behind the watering trough behind, and the stone well at the side, the dead piled up. But their number was not enough.

Magpie Myers had a savage rip along one arm, his old blood dripping like slow tropic rain on the floor. Bill Lang was hit in the shoulder. Ricardo, gray-faced and grim with pain and loss of blood from his leg wound, was hit across the face and in the side.

Pablo's neck was fountaining blood, though he was still at his window slinging careful, deadly lead at those men outside.

Lars Johanssen, bullet-careless, staggered like a stricken elephant and bellowed defiance like a fighting bull.

Bill Lang's thigh was punctured by a bullet that angled in

from a roof top. Only Jim Clane, his face flaming with the sheer joy of a fight, seemed unhurt.

Silver himself had taken a slug in the ribs, a slashing fire across the hips, and stunning crease along the scalp.

He shoved fresh cartridges into his hot guns and triggered coldly, seeing his lead strike home. But he knew that this was no use. They had come closer. It was a question of time—and damn little time.

Behind him, Pedro, the father of a fighting kid, was whimpering despairingly in a corner. But at Silver's elbow Maria's voice said, "Señor, here are two shotguns loaded. Ours and that of Carlos who owns this house. When they come closer—"

Silver swept the guns from her hands and pushed her aside. "You'll do, *madre*," he said. "You'll do plenty."

Bill Lang's snarling voice lifted, "The dirty crawling quitter! I knew damn' well he was a yeller-bellied greaser fake!"

Silver looked at him wonderingly, thinking at first that he was talking about Pedro Morales.

But Lang gestured savagely at the place where Pablo had been and then at a trapdoor in the ceiling. "Your knife-stickin' spick lieutenant that you think so much of. He's quit us!"

Lars Johanssen turned toward Lang with anger in his face, but Ricardo was nearest him. His knife gleamed in his hand, but then he slapped it grimly back into its sheath. "You damn lyin' greengo," he yelled. "Pablo ees more man than you will evair be!"

His fist shot out and missed Lang's dodging jaw. Then his leg gave under him and he plunged face-down onto the floor.

CHAPTER 5
GUN-DOCTOR
FOR THE DAMNED

A NOTHER SOUND interrupted. It was not a loud sound, and it should not have been heard over the storm of gunfire and the snarl of bullets which filled that room. It was the breath of Dr. Snaipo going out in a sigh of satisfaction.

"That was a very interesting case," Dr. Snaipo said complacently. "Very interesting." He rubbed his long-jointed, big-knuckled hands together. Silver whirled away from his window.

"Will he live?" he demanded harshly.

El Diablo's doctor looked at him in faint astonishment. "Live?" he repeated vaguely. "Why—oh, yes, he'll live now, all right." He washed his hands together in pure satisfaction. "Most interesting case. The sigmoid flexure—"

Silver's eyes slapped at him, stopping that speech by sheer impact. His powerful hands clenched into whitened knuckles. "You frozen devil!" he snarled.

Dr. Snaipo stared at him in dazed astonishment.

Silver whirled toward the boy. He was lying there, pale and breathing shallowly, but as Silver stepped up he began to moan, tossing his head from side to side, "Mother?" he muttered. "Mother?"

A bullet snarled past Silver's ear and lifted a scant lock from the balding head of the man before him. But the medico did not flinch. He seemed unaware of the death which had breathed its hornet breath against him.

Silver turned away from him with the sobbing sound of Maria's unutterable joy in his ears as she flung herself on her knees beside Pedrocito. He looked at Dr. Snaipo.

"I should not thank you, Doctor," he said quietly, "because I understand that you did none of this for me. But I thank you just the same. Name your price."

EL DIABLO'S physician seemed to grow an inch in height, so that he towered over Silver. "Money, señor?" he replied with overwhelming dignity. "No doubt you do not understand. I do not any longer take money for my work. I do not like you, señor, because you slapped my head against the wall. But money has nothing to do with that."

"In that case, Doctor," Silver managed to say evenly, "you are free to go. It would be best, also, if you went at once. If you wave a white flag out the door and then go out, they will no doubt recognize you and will not shoot at you. But before you go, I wish to offer you my apologies. I am very sorry that I slapped your head against the wall."

"Very well," the doctor said primly, "I accept your apology. But I assure you, my dear sir, that I have no intention of going out."

Silver felt suddenly a little insane. "I—I don't understand," he stammered. "But—but maybe you don't quite realize that our case here is hopeless. Anybody who's fool enough to—"

Dr. Snaipo waved at him impatiently. "I am vexed with Señor Bautista because he ordered his men to fire when I was busy," he explained. "I will tolerate no interruption to my work."

He swelled his long, chicken-breasted chest indignantly, and a bullet clipped a button off it.

Dr. Snaipo ignored it.

Silver swore softly in wonder. "Then—then—" he gulped, "you had better fight. Can you shoot at all?"

Dr. Snaipo stared at him. "They are fighting us?" he asked politely. "Of course I can shoot," he added as an afterthought. "It is a childish skill, but I have learned it in case of need." His enormously long, big-knuckled hand reached in under his coat and came out holding a revolver of obviously foreign make. "Besides," he said querulously, "I am very much vexed with Señor Bautista. He might have interrupted one of my most interesting cases."

Only then did Silver realize that he had altogether forgotten to search this man for weapons. Outside, the volume of fire suddenly redoubled.

"They're comin' in!" Magpie gasped.

Ricardo was still unconscious. Jim Clane was down, blood seeping from his scalp. Magpie, from exhaustion and loss of blood, was obviously weakening. Only Bill Lang and Lars were fit to fight.

Silver jumped to a window and saw that it did not matter much whether the others could fight or not. The broad street in front was swarming with their dodging, flame blasting figures. The alley way to the rear sounded their coming and as he watched he saw figures zigzagging over the flat roofs nearby.

It was the finish. This time he had counted too much on his luck. But despite the fact that he had sacrificed his men, he could not feel too much depression. At least, one gallant kid would get well, and that, somehow, seemed worth everything.

Methodically deadly, his guns began to hammer against his palms. Dodging figures jerked under the impact of his lead, went down or staggered backward. Only, one of them went down too fast, dying from a bullet which was not Silver's.

Instinctively he looked to see where the shot had come from, and then yelled. Dr. Snaipo was standing calmly in the window, his tall, gaunt form fully exposed, triggering his gun.

Outside, a hurtling figure checked, slapped the middle of his chest with his hand and plunged on his face. Dr. Snaipo frowned slightly, as a man does who has missed something that he ought to have hit.

Silver gulped involuntarily, and then threw back his head and laughed joyously aloud. At least Life had offered him this before he died!

BEFORE HE died? His eyes widened, abruptly attentive. Something was happening out there. A new storm of gunfire sounded. And El Diablo's men were suddenly like chickens confronted with a threat, running here and there in excited confusion.

And then the cause of their panic showed—a sudden phalanx, an army, was marching down that street with guns blazing.

And leading them were two people-Pablo, and a woman!

A broad-hipped, hard-striding, ax-faced woman, her white hair a confusion of flying tendrils in this dusky light, her clawed hands holding an ancient blasting sixgun.

For just one moment Silver stood motionless against the

135

frame of his window. He had endured a lot this day; and he was not altogether himself.

It flashed through his mind that Pablo had said, "It is the town of my aunt. She is called Tia Hacha, and once she was a great woman. But now she is old."

Tia Hacha—Aunt Ax!

But where was this terrified town? Where were these humble people who had paid tribute to El Diablo, and dared not brook his wrath?

Why, they were marching down this street with guns in their hands, in order that Silver Trent and his men—*Los Halcónes de las Sierras*—should not die!

Silver turned to Dr. Snaipo at the window to his right. "Friend," he said huskily, "all the miracles are not medical."

Dr. Snaipo stared at him without comprehension, not knowing that somehow Pablo had cursed courage into beaten men.

But Lars Johanssen bellowed his joy and plunged through the window. Bill Lang snarled like an elated wildcat as he followed.

Their racing, slamming guns put the final touch on the panic of the Bautista crowd. They broke and scattered. And Silver understood that this fight was all over.

The bulk of those tribute-paying townsmen spread out, howling in the pursuit of the fleeing minions of El Diablo, but Tia Hacha stomped up at Pablo's side to the window where Silver Trent stood.

Silver saw then that this woman was indeed ancient, her face a leathery mass of wrinkles, but her eyes were still alive.

"So!" she snapped in a voice which was tart for all its quavering "you are the great Hawk of the Sierras! In my day there lived men that might have made you look smaller. Still, I can thank you for what you have done this day."

Pablo cut in desperately, like a schoolboy whose parent disgraces him. *"Jefe!* This is my aunt. She is called Tia Hacha. Now she is old, and—"

"Quiet, boy!" the old woman cut in reprovingly. "Will you talk when your elders speak?"

Behind Silver, Magpie grinned feebly and Lars Johanssen shattered the twilight with a great guffaw. "Quiet, *niño!*" he yelled, and grabbed his stomach. "Haw! Haw! Haw! You batter quit talkin', *niño!*"

Pablo glared and grabbed at his knife, knowing that he, Pablo, who was old, maybe the next oldest to Magpie, would never live this down. But Tia Hacha ignored all this. She put a hand on her ancient hip and swaggered a little. "A proper man," she said to Silver. "I think my little Pablo is maybe almost as smart as he should be."

Silver bowed. "Tia Hacha," he said, "my life is a little thing to owe, but I am glad that I hold it by grace of such a woman as yourself. If I were a little more mature I would ask your hand in marriage."

Pablo's aunt cackled delightedly. "If I was six months younger," she creaked, "I'd make you a proposal wickeder than that! But something tells me now, *caballero mio,* that we of Villa Maria will pay no longer tribute to the Devil!"

Silver grinned at her ninety-odd years and said, "It would

have stopped long ago, had I known it was the town of Pablo's aunt!"

Dr. Snaipo cut in, leaning in the window beside Silver. "The young man who fainted, who tells me his name is Ricardo," the doctor said precisely, "is in no danger, though he has lost much blood and must have care. I do not see how he kept up so long as he did. The other, the red-haired one, was merely creased on the head. He cursed me, quite unnecessarily, while I was attending him. Their cases are without interest. I will go now."

Silver drew in a deep breath and turned to him. "Doctor," he murmured, "if you—are vexed with Bautista, why not stay with us? We have no money—" he hoped that he would be forgiven that bald-faced lie—"but...."

Snaipo gazed at him doubtfully. "I had considered it," he said, "but I would have to have complete liberty, and—and I am not sure that you could provide me with cases that—"

Silver cut in hastily. "Besides," he said, "you would have a confrere who is really a physician and a scientist. Someone with whom you could talk!"

Dr. Snaipo's face lighted up so that the glow seemed to come from all his great domed head. "A real physician? Not one of these small town Mexican idiots? Are you sure? I would accept...." He looked like a small, petulant boy who had gotten a totally unexpected and miraculous toy.

But behind Silver a small, faint clear voice lifted, "Madre—Madre—is he yet here, the Hawk? You promised—"

Silver turned, the movement of his great body somehow humble. "Yes, niño," he said gently, "I am here...."